The Seer's Stone

Mary Seaforth

By the same author:

The Watching Shadow
(Book II of the 'Seer' trilogy)
The Final Prophecy
(Book III of the 'Seer' trilogy)

The Seer's Stone

by

Mary Seaforth

Volume II

310 Kennington Road, London SE11 4LD

The characters in this book are imaginary.
No such person as my wholly fictional
Kenneth Mackenzie has ever,
to my knowledge, existed.

Printed and bound by B.W.D. Ltd. Northolt, Middx.
Issued by Volume II *
ISBN 1 85846 060 3
* An imprint of The Professional Authors' & Publishers' Association

ACKNOWLEDGEMENTS

My grateful thanks to Elizabeth Sutherland for her permission to borrow some of the characters from *The Seer of Kintail*. These characters, as well as providing the necessary links, have been the inspiration for this book and without them it would not have been possible.

My thanks also to Mrs Dorothy Child for her help and interest.

* * *

The cover photograph of Kenneth, 3rd Earl of Seaforth, is reproduced with the kind permission of Ross & Cromarty District Council

CONTENTS

Introduction

For those unfamiliar with the legend of Coinneach Odhar, otherwise known as the 'Brahan Seer' and the subject of my trilogy, the story of his short and ultimately tragic life is as follows.

Coinneach Odhar, meaning sallow or dull-coloured Kenneth, came from Baile na Cille on the Isle of Lewis in the middle - or thereabouts - of the seventeenth century. Making his way in stages through various parts of Scotland, prophesying as he travelled, he eventually, and at the behest of Kenneth, 3rd Earl of Seaforth, came to Brahan Castle.

Already his prophecies were widely known, especially in Lewis, Harris, Benbecula, Skye and Kintail, as well as the Black Isle, and already some of them had been fulfilled. Many more were to follow, including the one which prophesied the doom and final extinction of the Seaforth family: perhaps the strangest and most intriguing of them all, for the prophesy came true in every respect, but not until about one hundred and seventy years after its utterance, and even then it was not entirely fulfilled until 1966.

Now there are no Mackenzies of Seaforth at Brahan, and never will be again. How the final prophesy came about, and took so long to be fulfilled, is anyone's guess. Perhaps some day a true explanation will emerge: one which will prove conclusively that it did happen according to the legend.

All of Coinneach Odhar's prophecies were made with the help of his magic stone, given to him, so it is supposed, by his mother, who in her turn received it from the King of Norway's daughter* one night when in the graveyard at Baile na Cille tending the cattle in the summer pastures. Opinions

*See *The Seer of Kintail* by Elizabeth Sutherland

vary as to the colour, shape and size of the stone, but this does not matter. What does matter is that this strange young man, educated and shrewd, was completely under its influence; and though he never, as far as we know, did harm to anyone during his 'fits' of prophesying he could not have been completely sane, and eventually his 'seeings' proved his undoing.

The Seer stayed on at Brahan Castle for some time after the Earl had been summoned to France by the exiled king, Charles II, and with his strange ways Coinneach Odhar soon aroused the curiosity of the Earl's wife, Isabella.Whether or not she really wanted to know what her husband was up to at the French court, or whether she merely wanted an excuse to put the Seer through his paces is not known. Suffice that she asked for news of her lord and he refused to tell her. She insisted until finally he gave in and told her he had 'seen' her husband carousing at the French court with no thought for his wife left at home to manage his house and estates.

Isabella, not unnaturally furious, ordered the Seer to be thrown into a spiked tar-barrel which was to be set alight and burned at Chanonry Point in the Black Isle. Between her orders being given and carried out the Seer uttered his final prophesy, which is the title of the third book of my trilogy.

This, the first book, concerns itself with a fictional descendant of the family who finds the Seer's magic stone. It is meant to be a warning of the evil and dreadful results attendant upon the practice of 'stone worshipping' when carried to extreme lengths.

The second book, *The Watching Shadow* (whose title also comes from one of the Seer's prophesies), is an attempt to vindicate Isabella Seaforth's cruel and terrible deed - an action which was so foreign to her nature that she cannot, in my view, be held entirely responsible for it.

PART ONE

THE PROUD HIND

1663

Standing in the big hall of the castle they confront one another. She, known as the Tall Woman (amongst other things), playing laird in her husband's absence, is a gaunt but impressive figure in her mulberry and silver satin gown, a rope of large pearls round her neck, huge pearl drops in her ears and a brooch of three more set in a ruby bed pendant at her bosom. She has been sitting for Mr. Scougal, who is painting her likeness. Her light brown hair is dressed in ringlets and there is a gold fillet threaded through them. She stands with her hands folded, looking down her long bony nose at the man before her.

He looks back thoughtfully, his gaze not insolent but not subservient either. Not respectful enough, she is thinking furiously. For all that he is of my lord's finding and his creature, yet he is *my* servant and he will obey me.

This is not their first meeting. Already this uncomfortable person has been at the castle for several months and has not, as my lady Isabella desired, accompanied her lord to Paris.

She has summoned him, but now he has arrived she does not know what to say to him. She wishes for news of her lord (whom she does not trust and with good reason) but the quietly dressed young man standing almost respectfully before her will not give her what she desires. He has so said he does not know many times ... "But you can 'see'" she cries in exasperation. "You are a prophet, a seer; why can you not 'see' my lord at the French Court?"

1

His eyes drop before her angry gaze. He bows slightly and takes a step backwards. Then he raises his eyes to hers and in them she detects a mocking look. It is too much. Furiously she turns on her heel and returns to her retiring room to wrestle once more with her lord's curious accounting system.

But once there she takes no interest in the papers scattered all over her bureau. Instead she sits down; examines her hands, bites her nails savagely, scowls angrily and exclaims aloud: "By all the Saints! What ails me?" Then she jumps up and, grinding her teeth, strikes at the mass of papers on the bureau, sending most of them onto the floor.

What ails her? She knows the answer too well. She wants a man; not just any man; not a drunken sot like her lord but the Seer himself. She hates him; she is in awe of him, especially when he 'sees' ... but she wants him.

She strides to the fireplace, tugs at a rope and sets a bell clanging in the bowels of the huge castle. Her woman, Agnes, arrives at a gallop. She looks scared and flustered.

"My lady?" She curtseys clumsily.

"Bring me that man. The Seer as he designates himself. Bring me Coinneach Odhar. Tell him he is to help me with these;" and she waves her hand at the scattered papers on the floor.

"Shall I pick them up?" asks Agnes.

"No. He who calls himself the Seer, who is above menial tasks ... he can prostrate himself before me and perform this one. For what do you wait, wench? Go ... and hurry."

Presently she hears his footfall outside the door and a knock. Agnes precedes him and steps aside for him to enter, but she does not curtsey.

"You sent for me?"

"Yes. I need help with these cursed accounts. Agnes, you may go ... and tell Master Videl I shall not require him

2

today. Tell him ... tell him what you like ... that I am indisposed."
(I do not like him, though his prating diverts me. To myself I
call him the Black Priest. But this man, the Seer, sets me afire.)

She turns to the Seer.

"Now, great Seer, let us see if your talents can be used in
a fruitful cause. Pick up all those papers, put them in order,
make a tally of the sums therein and give me the total
reckonings."

He does as he is bid without a word. (I watch him, a
perfect volcano of lust and longing rising up in me until I feel I
must burst. I am mad for him ... so much so that if I were the
man I should have been and he the woman, I should take him
here ... now, as he doubtless takes that drab who visits him in
his bothy.) She continues to watch him avidly, her strange
yellow-brown eyes glowing.

By sundown Coinneach Odhar has settled the matter
relating to the estate and presents the Countess with the
reckoning. She checks it twice, thrice, but can find no fault.
The work is finished; she can no longer keep him by her side.

"You may go," she says at last. "I thank you; you are
clever with figures." He bows and goes towards the door. She
racks her brains in desperation for an excuse to see him again
... alone.

"Stay!" she commands. "There is the matter of a bothy
which my lord would have me build at the end of the west
carriage drive. The estate has need of a further grieve to tend
the pasture. It is too large an area for the grieves of the castle
bothies, nor is there another between. You shall advise me as
to its situation. Be there at noon on the morrow. Tell Agnes to
order my pony."

The following morning Agnes dresses her in her green
velvet habit and places a bonnet with an eagle's feather in it on

3

her yellow-brown hair. She descends the Great Staircase, whip in hand, and takes her place in the saddle, impatiently waving aside the serving man who would go with her.

"I want no company. I shall return within the hour," she tells him.

Coinneach Odhar is there waiting at the end of the long carriage drive. He helps her dismount and ties her pony's reins to the branch of a tree. He waits for her to speak. It is at this point that Isabella somewhat loses her head. (At last, at last we are alone. Now, great Seer, let us discover if you make love as well as you untangle accounts.) She moves closer to him drifting her hands across his shoulders. Her body is on fire and he senses it. He begins to breathe hard; she is after all a young woman and for some time now he has had no wench, his companion of the bothy having deserted him for another man.

He takes her outstretched hands and draws her to him. She sinks down, down into the bracken out of sight though they are quite safe. No one ever comes that way. He too sinks into the bracken beside her. Darkness engulfs them.

Once more she is alone in her retiring room. It is many days since she has set eyes on Coinneach Odhar and her briefly assuaged lust is now upon her again, fiercer than ever.

"Agnes?"

"Yes, my lady?"

"I would visit the place for the new bothy again. Tell the Seer to be there at noon on the morrow; and tell them I shall want my pony."

On this day the auguries are less good. Half way along the drive it starts to rain. When she gets to the end he is waiting. He steps forward to take the bridle. She moves as though to dismount, but he forestalls her, holding up his hand.

"My lady. There can be no repeat of your last visit here. We have done my lord a great wrong. I cannot deceive him again."

"Of course," she prevaricates, dismounting."It is raining. Let us choose another day and somewhere to ... "

"No. No ... and again no." He is in great agitation - not looking at her. But she recognises the signs. (He is at that ... his prophesying ... again. An excuse? No. He spurns me then?) She watches him, a look of anger on her face and indeed he has the Stone in his hand, which is clenching itself upon it. He looks strained and beads of sweat stand out on his forehead.

"What ails you, man?" she cries. And as he makes no answer she steps forward raising her whip. "Heed me when I speak to you." But he is muttering low beneath his breath and she cannot hear him. All at once she feels an evil presence at hand though whether it emanates from the man himself or his instrument, she cannot tell; nor even if the two are divisible. A little afraid, for all her anger, she taps him on the shoulder with her whip. He turns to her and his face is normal again, the Stone back in his pocket.

"You were 'seeing' were you not?" she asks curiously. "Tell me what you 'saw'."

" 'Twas nothing. But an idea; not a clear vision."

"What? I demand to know."

"On the spot where your horse is standing, some time in the future; ... something will occur."

"What manner of thing?"

"I know not. I did not 'see' it properly. Perhaps a death. I know not," he repeats.

"Does it concern my family?"

"It does. It may be part of a 'seeing' which is to come. And now I must bid you good day." He steps back, bows slightly

5

and vanishes into the tall bracken.

(Now I can find no further excuse to bring him to me. My accounts are in order; he will not take me for his mistress nor will I beg it of him. Isabella, the Proud Hind does not beg favours from a servant, like a whore from the bothies. But stay ... he has not yet given me news of my lord).

She sends for Coinneach Odhar a third time.

He comes to her. She commands him to tell her what he "sees" of her lord and his doings. He refuses and prepares to leave her. She is too quick for him and she rushes to the door barring his passage. He puts her gently aside, searching her face, his expression pitying; rather sad. All her anger leaves her.

"What would you hear of your lord?" he asks. "That he is dead?"

"The truth, Coinneach Odhar. The truth."

"I do not know what is the truth. My 'seeing' cannot encompass the wide water that lies between us and France. I cannot help you. I only know that ... " He hesitates.

"Yes?"

"That he is well and happy." And with these words he is gone. She knows that he is lying; that there is more.

"Agnes?"
"Yes, my lady?"
"Send for Master Videl."
"Yes, my lady."

The Black Priest comes in softly. He does everything softly. Even his hands are soft and white. I fear him; I know not why. And why did he not accompany the Bishop, long since

6

departed? Both were paying a visit in my lord's presence. The visit of Master Videl has much prolonged itself. The Bishop's too was overlong.

I look at him as he approaches me (softly). I mistrust as well as fear him now. I suspect him of dallying with souls - with the Seer's soul. And with mine. But I must know what to do. He comes close to me and the hair rises on my scalp. I feel cold. My flesh shrinks at his nearness. All at once a light is lit in my mind. If Coinneach Odhar's Stone were in the soft hands of the Black Priest, would evil result from the contact? I think it would. I ask myself, is the evil there already in each one of us or can a little stone hold all that I sense in this man, Master Videl? It overcomes the Seer but he does not always see evil happenings and I am convinced he is no slave to Satan. Were I in possession of the Stone, should I be overcome? Foretell evil happenings? Perhaps commit some dreadful deed? I shudder, either with cold at the nearness of the Black Priest or at my own wicked thoughts. For this is witchcraft. I must not dwell upon such matters.

He seems to sense my malaise ... and read my thoughts.

"My lady. Is it true, think you, that the Seer practises Witchcraft?"

I laugh lightly. "You voice my own thoughts, Master Videl. I am not in his confidence. And you? You know nothing?" (Yet you are after his soul, I am persuaded. If not his soul, the Stone, which is perhaps the same thing.)

"No, madam. He tells me nothing." (And yet Agnes reports visits to the bothy where he dwells. On what do they discourse then? Midwifery?)

There is a silence. The Black Priest watches her maliciously.

"My lady. You wished to see me?" he prompts. He sounds tense and expectant.

7

"Yes. I would have news of my lord. The Seer tells me he is well and happy, but there is something other that he will not tell me. I know he has the means, but he will not use them."

"Perhaps he dare not admit to the Black Arts, my lady."

"To me?"

"To you or anyone." (Yet he already has to me and it was nonsense. It meant nothing. How can he see so far into the future?)

"But the 'seeings' are widely known and believed ... by those of few wits."

"Ay, my lady; but no harm comes from them ... yet."

"And this ... ? If he 'sees' my lord? Will this be harmful?"

"It is possible."

"What then shall I do?"

"Leave it to me, madam. Betimes, forget the Seer. Cause a great Feast to be held in honour of your birthday. Invite the kinsmen and the Clan. Before the Feast is over you shall have your answer."

"You will not harm him?"

"Not one hair of his head." (But his soul ... his soul?)

(Yet the Seer *shall* tell me that which I wish to know ... must know ... even if he loses both his soul and his life. My mind is made up. He has spurned me and refused to obey my commands. Now he will refuse me no longer. I am determined to humiliate him, even as he has humiliated me. But I love him. I want him. I cannot be the instrument of his death.)

The Feast is over. There was a new reel danced in my honour and I drank deeply. It was a happy evening ... until the Seer joined us. My neighbour, Fairburn, would have me ignore the man, but Master Videl's eyes were upon me and I could not but know that something was about to occur.

8

An immensely tall man, the Black Priest, and as he stepped forward a hush fell upon the gathering so that all were silent.

"Good-day to you, Seer," he cried, his pale eyes now fixed upon Coinneach. "On this festive occasion let us have a little diversion. We who have heard of your wondrous 'seeings' would now wish you to perform one for us so that we may behold a true prophet for ourselves. You must know," he continued, "that my lady Isabella needs news of her lord, gone from here for so many months now. She knows he is well and happy for she heard this of him. But you, who are acclaimed for your sage prophecies and findings ... you know more which you would conceal from her. Come now, man, take out your magic stone and tell us what we need to know." His traitorous eyes were now fixed on me, cold, cunning, evil. I felt a strange compulsion. I stepped forward.

"Yes," I said. "Do as Master Videl bids you ... or we shall think your prophecies to be the mere tricks of a charlatan and there is no truth in them. Come now. What are you? A true Seer or are you practising witchcraft with evil intent?"

At the word witchcraft a great gasp rose from the assembled company. "Yes," I repeated. "Witchcraft ... for which the penalty is death? So, Seer, will you answer me now? What news have you of my lord. Does he think of me on this day?"

(God forgive me. There is no return for either of us now.)

Coinneach Odhar's hand was working on the Stone. His eyes were blank and distant, glassy as a loch on a still day, and when he spoke his voice was low, seeming to come from another world.

"Come now," I said again and stamped my foot imperiously. "The news of my lord, if you please."

"If you will, madam. I can gainsay you no longer. So be it then. Your lord has not thought of you this day nor for many days past. He too is occupied with feasting and dancing. I see

9

him in a gold room and he too is dressed in gold. There is a *beautiful* lady with him and his arm is about her shoulders. He whispers in her ear and they laugh together."

"You lie, Seer," I cried with shaking voice, though my body was frozen with shock. "My lord would never serve me thus." Now I was shaking all over with anger - not at my lord and his wenching - (there is nothing new about that) - but at the slight but meaning emphasis I thought Coinneach Odhar to have put upon the word 'beautiful'. I know so well that I am not. Was I not known, at first anyway, as my lord's plain bride? It is true my nose is like a skua's beak; my eyes are pale as are my lashes and brows. But to hear this slight ... this insult pronounced before all my guests ... oh, he shall repent this. By all the Saints he shall repent.

Even so I was not prepared for what was to follow.

Seeing my hesitation, the Black Priest stepped forward again and when he spoke his voice was smooth and cold.

"Seer," he proclaimed. "You have insulted a lady with your lying accusations. What you have just purported to 'see' cannot be true. Were your 'seeings' to continue in their former childish vein, matters might have been different. But you have used a tool of the Devil for the purpose of harm. You are not, as I suspected, a mere charlatan; your prophecies are scurrilous and evil and therefore a charge of witchcraft shall be incurred upon you." And before I could well stop him, he had stepped to the door and two guards (whom I now suspect had received orders to be standing ready outside) laid rough hands on Coinneach and dragged him away.

Somehow, later, I got rid of my company and though it was past midnight I summoned Master Videl.

"You have acted strangely tonight," I told him angrily as he came through the door. "How dare you order my guards to seize Coinneach Odhar without my permission? Answer me!"

10

He came closer and as always when in his presence, I grew cold.

"I ask your pardon, madam," he answered smoothly. "If I acted against your wishes, it was but with a desire to protect you." (Protect me? From what?) He continued: "Observing your hesitation, I feared that should you not take action with due swiftness against the man who said this wicked thing about your lord, a feeling of doubt might spread through the company. 'Why does she hesitate?' they might secretly have asked themselves; and further 'she is angry with the Seer, but she is not angry enough.' Forgive me, madam, but there is so much that might have entered their evil minds." (Even more than that which entered yours? I think not.) He stopped and eyed me slyly.

Now I understood. Why did he not voice his own thought - What is that man to her? He was clearly in a ferment to know.

"Such hesitation, my lady," he continued, "could have been most dangerous. Once the word witchcraft had been uttered ... for witchcraft it is ... could it not have been thought that you were implicated?"

He is so cruelly clever ... so cunning. Now I really fear him, for he is right. I cannot defend Coinneach, now or ever. The charge of witchcraft if proved (and the Black Priest will prove it as surely as God is in Heaven and I am already in Hell), means death for both of us. How can I, Isabella, Countess of Seaforth, admit myself as conspiring in witchcraft? I cannot.

Now there is a new soul in the Black Priest's keeping. Mine. He has been after it for a long while now. And what of the other? Has he it yet? Perhaps not, but he will ... he will when he obtains possession of the Stone.

What have I done? Oh, what have I done?

11

I must see Coinneach. Alone. But how to contrive?

Agnes has bribed the guards with silver pieces taken from my lord's place of safe-keeping to which only I have the key. There were not many left, but I am to go tonight to the dungeons half after midnight when the castle sleeps. If I can only but tell Coinneach that I had no part in this.

It is all over. I have seen him ... or rather, I have heard him speak. It was so dark and all that could be seen by the rushlight carried by Agnes (who I suspect of lying with one of the guards) were the iron bars behind which he is confined.

We approached carefully, fearful of a sudden appearance of Master Videl. This would not have surprised me; his long nose is into everything. I thought I heard a faint rustling as we came nigh to the bars of the cell, but t'was only the wind over the grass.

I spoke very low.

"Coinneach Odhar ... it is I, ... " I could not say 'The Countess'. After all, had I not lain in his arms? In a fit of pettishness I nearly announced myself as 'Seaforth's plain wife' but neither could I taunt him with that which he had perhaps never meant to say. It is my doing that he is here now. I must not cause him more harm. So I announced myself as Isabella Seaforth quite simply and waited for the answer.

It came soon enough and by the tone of his voice I knew he was in the throes and that I was of no more interest to him than a rat in his cell. Most likely less ... and the words he spoke were very strange:

"Listen well," he said. "For what has been done this day and for what is to follow, your race will end though mine will continue. After I am dead, a child of my seed will be born on Brahan land and from his seed there will be one in every generation who will 'see' as I have seen; and let those beware who would do them harm, for my shadow will be watching over them."

What could this purport? What does he know that I do not? But the spirits of the night were abroad and God knows what witchcraft - and there has been talk enough of witchcraft.

Coinneach Odhar still has the Stone; but oh, that I had not insisted, like a nagging wife, for the news of my lord.

Today came the Black Priest, soft-footed as ever and with his large white hand took from beneath his cloak a crude figure of clay. A kind of doll clad in two scraps of mulberry and silver satin (had Agnes some part in this?) from the gown in which I am having my likeness taken by Mr. Scougal, and for which I have a fondness, since it becomes me as none of my others. My heart beat fast for I recognised myself in this witchen figure, and looking closer, I perceived a large thorn embedded in the region of the heart. I tried to laugh, but the Black Priest stayed me.

"My lady. I brought this to you since it is proof."

"Of what is it proof?" I asked, pretending innocence; trying in my turn to stay the Black Priest.

"It is proof of witchcraft. It was found in the Seer's bothy. The Witch of Ferintosh, once whore to the seer, put it there." (Did he then spurn her too? What manner of woman is she, who can use her own powers to send a man to his death? For proof it is. Incontrovertible.) He was speaking again, and there was a trace of elation in the oily tones. "Yes, madam. Should the kinsmen not prove to be satisfactory witnesses we shall need this." He pointed to the figure on the table. "With it we are certain beyond doubt that Coinneach Odhar is the tool of Satan. Not just Seer, prophet and charlatan, but active in evil and witchcraft." He saw me look doubtfully at the figure. Perhaps I made a move towards it for he snatched it up, wrapped it in his kerchief and concealed it once more in the folds of his cloak. Then he came a little closer and there was that in his eyes which filled me with cold dread.

"Do you remember what I told you at the Feast, madam? That there are those who wish you harm; who think you have had some part in this? ... " (Some tacksmen evicted for bad husbandry, does he mean? Yet who would take their word against that of the kinsmen and myself?) "... Those who may even think ... "

"That I am the mistress of the Seer, and an adulteress!" I cried beside myself. "Is that what they think?"

He bowed, but did not deny it.

"Go," I shouted furiously. "Go from here. Are you so innocent as not to perceive ... ?" I was suddenly tired of it all. "Do what you will with the man," I called after his retreating figure. "I am no accomplice of his nor is his presence in the castle of my seeking ... "

He turned to look once more at me with slate-cold eyes. Could I but have seen them more clearly I would have known they reflected his feeling of sly satisfaction. Oh yes, he has got the better of us all. He closed the door softly and there was even menace in the sound of the falling latch.

I know now the purport of Coinneach's strange prophecy. I am with child. I know too (since my lord has been gone these five months) that a spell beyond even the Seer, whose babe it is, cannot arrange matters in time for me to father it upon my lord. Perhaps I will miscarry. Should I not, no one but Agnes must know, and when my time comes she must take it for her own and find some woman to wet-nurse it. For I cannot acknowledge it. It can never know me for its mother. Is

Coinneach Odhar to know? If I can but contrive a meeting alone with him, I must tell him. He will not betray me and it will not seem untoward if I visit him, as would my lord were he here (though were he in his rightful place there would be no need ... no misbegotten child either.) On the eve of the trial I will visit Coinneach in the dungeons where he rots awaiting his cruel and undeserved fate.

They would not let me see him. Now he will never know.

The day of the trial I shall remember till my death for all that the last words - the curse - of Coinnneach Odhar do not ring as loudly in my ears as do his screams.

I pleaded illness and indeed I felt ill, but I am required by law to be present to testify ... to testify to what? All eyes are upon me as the Charge is read. It comes across to me in snatches as I feel my mind wandering; my wits astray.

"Coinneach Odhar, you are indicted and accused by Isabella Seaforth of ... that you did practise to deceive and injure ... witchcraft ... prophecy ... diabolic incantation ... did attempt to estrange ... her most noble lord ... and did consort with other witches."

But I said none of these things. This is the foul work of the Black Priest acting as intermediary; seeking through me, as though to carry out my wishes, to have my poor Seer indicted and found guilty of witchcraft. He, the Black Priest, wants the Stone so he can procure his own magic; so people will hearken unto him and believe in his as they do the Seer's. Above all he wants the Seer's soul as he has mine. Are two souls so much better than one? And will the magic of the Stone work for him?

"How say you, prisoner? Guilty, or not guilty?" But I

15

cannot hear the reply. Perhaps there was none.

The Black Priest steps forward. He pushes the Seer's hand aside to reveal the Stone and cries out: "Let him die the Death!"

All eyes are upon me. "The Death ... " I hear myself utter as though from very far away. A sudden swoon overcomes me. "What have I said?" I hear myself asking as arms support me and a goblet of wine is held to my lips. I know without seeing that it is the Black Priest who succours me, so assiduous as he is ... so determined that my name and not his will go down the years - perhaps into the history books of Scotland - as the murderer of the Seer. I, Isabella, am to be the accredited murderer of Coinneach Odhar, the Brahan Seer. Seaforth's plain bride: The Tall Woman: so am I variously described. Add to these attributes a vindictive nature, a sharp tongue and sarcastic wit and I am a sorry figure. Why does the Black Priest make me do this dreadful thing? Why does he hate me so? And to what end? What does he want of me? He cannot want my body. He is vowed to celibacy and even if he were not, no man other than Seaforth has ever wanted that (and to Seaforth I suspect one woman is as like unto another as eggs in a nest). My soul he has already and now he has got the Stone - the ultimate means whereby he can wield the power he craves.

And then I hear, as clear as the waves breaking on the Ness, the voice of Coinneach Odhar: "Woman," he cries, as though he too were not almost at his last gasp: "Heed me well for I see far into the future where lies the doom of the House of Seaforth. Mackenzie to Mackenzie, Kintail to Kintail, Seaforth to Seaforth, all will end in extinction and sorrow. I see a chief, the last of his house, and he is both deaf and dumb. He will be father to four fine sons but he will follow them all to

16

the grave. He will live in sorrow and die in mourning, knowing that the honours of his line are extinguished forever and that no future chief of Mackenzie shall ever rule in Kintail. Lamenting the last of his sons, he shall sink in sorrow to the tomb and the last of his possessions shall be inherited by a widow from the east who will kill her own sister."

Now I can keep silence no longer. This dreadful wicked curse he has put upon my descendants consumes me with passion indeed but less so than his treatment of me. He has taunted me; he has insulted and spurned me and now he addresses me as though I were his strumpet. At this moment I am afire with hate. And yet when I speak my voice is weak, low and full of pain. (As ever the Black Priest is close to my side but I heed him not.) "So many lies, Seer," I hear myself say, but so faintly I doubt if he can hear me. "All your prophesies are lies, Coinneach Odhar. You will burn in Hell in the pitch and no one can save you."

He hears me.

"I am no liar," he says. "And as a sign that I speak the truth, look up at yonder birds."

I look to the sky. I see two birds - one a raven, the other a dove - circling the pyre which will consume his poor remains after the execution.

"One of those birds will return after my body is consumed. If the dove lights on the ashes and is consumed likewise, I am guilty; but if it be the raven that alights, then your Soul, woman, is in peril."

Another swoon comes upon me and I begin to slip away, but cannot outdistance the screams of agony. Why the screams? A man does not scream as the hangman's noose tightens around his neck. He cannot utter. I open my eyes. I see the Black

Priest.

"Your commands have been carried out, madam."

"My commands? I gave none."

"My lady, you said to him he would burn in Hell - in the pitch - and that is what has been done. Your voice was faint, but I leant close lest I should fail to hear your words."

"'Tis you, not him, who is servant of the Devil?" I cry, distraught, " ... for all that you live and dress so saintly ... "

"Madam," he says warningly. "Heed what you say to me. I know your secret. You could still go the same way ... with him into Hell."

But I can stand no more. I rise and distance myself from him ... afraid lest I utter that which will be my undoing as well as Coinneach Odhar's. And I have done nothing to try and save him. I cannot.

I hear a great shouting. I look round and perceive my lord, of all people, his wig awry; his face the colour of the mulberry of my gown. He is proceeding at a pace which must surely bring upon him an apoplexy were he to continue in this fashion. And why is he not mounted? Belike he has ridden his poor horse to death as he does to so many when in his cups. I turn away. I wish he were gone, so weary am I of them all. Yet he is here and now I must play the temptress. Tonight, and for as many nights as it takes to get him into bed before his sottishness overcomes him. Once he has sown his seed in me I can bring forth this child (for all that it will look over large for one that lacks a few weeks in the womb) and none can then say I have fathered it on any other than my husband. Nor will my lord notice. He has already sons who bear his name and are his. No. Better far he should know nothing. Yet ... there might be gossip. The Black Priest? He suspects ...

I can do nothing for you, Seer. Once you had uttered the final prediction, no one could save you.

I will watch over your son.

Forgive me, Coinneach Odhar.

PART TWO

ISABELLA

1943

The main gates, flanked by a lodge and a bronze stag on each of the pillars were long since left behind. Now the stately beech trees had given way to tightly-packed conifers, as tall as the beeches but with dark green foliage overlapping, letting little, and in some places, no light at all, filter through onto the pot-holed drive.

Isabella Mackenzie swore, slapped at a swarm of flies, wiped her forehead with her hair and went stolidly on. Her sole companion was a middle-aged bicycle, a spinsterish Raleigh which had already travelled many miles and was as indispensable to Isabella as to every other adventurous girl in petrol-starved Britain ... and it was because of this bicycle for which there had been no room in the overloaded car that she was making the journey, mostly on foot, from the station, uphill all the way including the four-mile drive.

"At any moment now ... very, very soon I shall see it. The castle. *My* castle," said Isabella delightedly to her bicycle.

It was an unusual situation for a girl of Isabella's age to find herself in. Her father, member of a cadet clan and a cousin, was also a Mackenzie as had been her mother before her marriage; as would the next owner be obliged to call themselves, whatever their original name. He was already dead, Isabella's father, an early casualty at sea together with his entire ship's company. He and her mother divorced before the war; she almost immediately married a Frenchman and went to live in France and was there when the Germans invaded. Both she and her husband lost no time in organising a Resistance group and by now had more or less vanished from Isabella's life. Occasionally brief coded messages were received, but all that the girl really knew about her mother was that she was still, in 1943, alive.

After the divorce the child was sent to live with her father's only sister, Aunt Kitty, her husband and two daughters in Surrey. The three girls were of an age and went to the same school. There, any similarity between them ended. The cousins were bouncy, uninhibited girls who grew up liking all the usual things; parties, clothes, make-up; men. Especially men; discussed endlessly in giggling whispers and much implied knowledge by two bird-brained girls who never read a book if they could go to the cinema (and sometimes bicycled many miles in order to do so). Their knowledge of 'love' was as limited as Isabella's own - which was how she intended it to remain.

She was altogether different; a strange girl. Tall, pale and bony; undeveloped even at seventeen, she had a great deal of light, gold-brown hair, her only beauty. Otherwise she was plain, sometimes ugly, with large light-green eyes, almost invisible eyelashes and brows and a nose like a buttress which continued on down her face forever. Later she might be handsome, but now she resembled a young skua and people were inclined to keep clear of her. Her aunt called her touchy. Her uncle, a kindly, rather persecuted little man, called her

21

serious-minded. But she wasn't. Behind the unprepossessing exterior there was a romantic soul and these are particularly difficult to pair off - a virtually impossible feat in wartime, however promising the material. Isabella, anything but promising material, hated men, parties, and organised activity - in that order and would stand about dance floors glowering like a Medusa, glum and sour. Her intellectual appearance was misleading for she read nothing but novels, which she devoured as fast as the library in Godalming could provide them.

These summer holidays had produced a truly splendid invitation to the three girls from a friend of Aunt Kitty's with a grand country-house which they had so far managed to keep going in spite of the war. The two sons of the house were to be on leave together and there was bound to be much jollification; picnics, parties and bathing. The cousins were delighted. Isabella was not. Nor was her aunt. She would have liked a short holiday from her niece. Like her daughters she was tired of the girl's long, glum face, her often surly manners and continual refusal to be jolly. It never occurred to her that the fatherless, virtually orphaned girl was in need of more than just enough to eat and a roof over her head. Aunt Kitty's family came a barely tolerated second to her war work anyway. Meanwhile there were all those labels to stick on Red Cross parcels for refugees. Forgetting Isabella she bustled away.

She was not allowed to forget her for long. Both her daughters came to her with complaints and lamentations about their cousin; sure that she would ruin their holiday.

"Oh Mummee, *must* she come?" they wailed. "She's such a drip and she's always got the curse and ... oh, she'll spoil everything. Can't she go to ... to ... Scotland or somewhere? She's always talking about that castle of hers." Thinking about it, the idea seemed attractive to Aunt Kitty.

It was true that Isabella was badly affected by this ritual blood shedding which over the years had come to assume an almost malignant significance. It visited her remorselessly every three weeks, lasted a week and the build-up was a sort of amassing of evil forces within her with herself as the ultimate sacrifice, though why she should be sacrificed and who to remained a mystery. But there was this ... balloon feeling; of something swelling up inside her and if the pressure wasn't released she would burst. Then when it did, there was the embarrassment and the discomfort of having to be padded until she could hardly walk, all of which took much time in the one bathroom and caused even more animosity. Visits to the chemist were a nightmare. She would hover in Boots, pretending to inspect make-up; prepared to wait forever missing the bus; having to walk all the way back if necessary, if only the man would go away and send a woman assistant to deal with her. Then the emergence into the street, scarlet-faced, clutching a bulky parcel, noting with envy the smug bulges in her cousins' mackintosh pockets. As she grew older she came to hate her beastly body, trying to ignore it where the cousins were forever admiring and basting theirs with strange concoctions. And after ... after things had calmed down she would be left feeling weak and depressed. She was, of course, painfully anaemic and her Aunt should have seen it, but the business had never bothered her, nor her daughters either, and she could see no reason why it should bother anyone else. To her it was just another of those weaknesses to which women are prone and have to put up with. *She* could forget it was happening; Isabella couldn't and it didn't make her any easier to live with.

The idea of Scotland came at a good moment. Isabella was just recovering from an unusually severe infliction but the news that she was to go home as *she* always thought of it cheered her wonderfully and her uncle was told-off to make the necessary arrangements. Obviously the girl could not sleep alone in an empty castle (though for all they knew it could still be occupied by the military) but there was no reason why the factor and his wife shouldn't accommodate her for a fortnight - which is why Isabella was pushing her bicycle up the drive of her mother's castle on a sultry morning in July.

At last the drive seemed to be levelling out. The trees were not so closely packed and from where she was standing, at a bend in the drive, she could make out the lines of a long roof, still a mile or more distant.

Tired of pushing she got onto the bicycle and, pedalling along the grassy strip at the edge of the drive, she managed to avoid the worst of the pot-holes - one had to be so careful of one's tyres these days. But now, at last, she was near the end of her journey. She rode past another lodge where washing hung limply from a line and a baby squalled and kicked at the sides of its pram. Here the road divided and a turning to the right ran along the side of a brick wall behind which was a vegetable garden of some size, situated, as is customary in Scotland, as far from the house as to cause maximum inconvenience to those who had to do with it.

But Isabella was not interested in the garden behind the wall. Her heart was pounding with excitement and unaccustomed exercise. She went straight on, forgetting that she was hot, dirty and sweaty and had spent the night in the luggage-rack of a third-class smoking compartment surrounded by soldiers who seemed not to want to sleep and who conversed in what was apparently a foreign language with occasional English words. Another moment and she was standing on the huge circular sweep of gravel, gazing up at her ancestral home and experiencing some quite acute twinges of disappointment.

No battlements, towers with loopholes, bastions and so on adorned this castle. There was, it was a true, a vestigial moat, but no drawbridge, portcullis nor other obvious signs of fortification ornamented one of the ugliest buildings she had ever seen. This could be no one's idea of a castle, least of all hers, already somewhat disillusioned to find it was in the middle of civilisation, only thirty miles from Inverness, instead of on an island in the middle of a wild loch, or a lonely outpost upon a rock pounded by gigantic waves guarding the western shore. Little did she know ... then ... how much history was enshrined within those ancient walls. All she could think of was that it looked like a barracks, which was bright of her, because that was what it had been used for at least twice in its long life. Until quite recently it had served as an officers' mess for the Norwegian army. And it was bigger, much bigger than she had imagined. It sprawled and stretched out behind half-way up to another steep incline. There seemed to be an acre at least of roof, more or less covered with huge slates, each the size of an ordinary window pane ... large, that is. But not even some rather insignificant crenellations on the east side could entirely remove the resemblance to a barracks.

As she stared, the old Vauxhall which had met her at the station drove up and Mr. Angus Stewart, the factor, got out.

"Sae ye got here at last," he said in a strong Lowland accent. "What do ye think on it, or hae ye no had the time to decide? It's no verra beautiful but it's fine inside, or was until the meelitary took it ower. Noo let me tak ye hame to meet Alison - ma wife - and we'll a' hae a wee bit dinner and then I'll tak ye roond the place. Och. let yon bicycle bide. It'll tak' nae harm; I'll pit it up agin the wa'."

They drove past what must once have been several fine lawns - now hayfields - with here and there a Nissen hut and various items of abandoned military paraphernalia and drew up at the front of another lodge at the entrance of another drive, where Mrs. Stewart was waiting for them. A little later they were sitting down to food such as Isabella, goggling impolitely and unbelievingly, had not seen for a very long time and could hardly remember, the roast chicken, bacon, sausages and bread sauce having been replaced by a dreary and unhealthy compulsory diet of fried bread and tomatoes, baked beans with the occasion bit of dry bacon and gristly sausage; leavened from time to time with a bit of fried Spam when they were lucky. This was really special and Alison Stewart had been to some trouble to get together a feast worthy of her young guest.

As round as the scones and usually as floury as the baps and bannocks she was forever baking and, unlike her husband, Alison was a Highlander, a Mackintosh from Moy, just outside Inverness, and very much easier to understand than her Lowland-speaking husband. They were childless but clearly devoted to each other.

Isabella ate an enormous lunch, politely refusing the strong black tea which normally accompanies any such feast in Scotland. Alison wouldn't let her help with the washing-up, sensing from the slight though well-brought-up hesitation with which the girl made her offer, that a holiday from this would be welcome. And as Angus had to see a tenant whose steading had partly collapsed in a gale, they went off as soon as he had consumed his black stewed tea to look round the castle, collecting a key at least three inches long from its hook in the estate office. She would have preferred to go alone and he must have sensed this for he said, as they drew up at the front: "I'll tak ye in and show ye where it isna' wise tae tread. The flair is nae ower strong in parts. And I'll see that the rooms ye'll be wanting tae veesit are nae lockit up. Syne I'll leave ye tae find yer way aboot, Miss Isabella." He led her up the steps which in turn led to a verandah and inserted the big key into the lock.

She looked back over her shoulder to the great sweep of lawn falling away to the river; to huge trees and a vast blue distance. Then Mr. Stewart gave the door a shove, stood back for her to pass and Isabella stepped over the threshold, suppressing a strong inclination (conscious of the factor close behind her) to jump up and tweak the straggly beard of one of the gnus which hung on either side of the door leading to the Great Hall.

1947

Isabella gazed down from 15,000 feet onto a completely white land. So much snow had fallen during that winter that only by the presence of bluish shadows was it possible to distinguish the lower hills of the Grampians from the flatter surfaces. It was terribly cold in the slow, underpowered clumsy old Oxford now on its way back from her Fleet Air Arm station near Edinburgh to its own base at Evanton.

She had the Oxford and its pilot to thank for that lift as most of the roads were blocked with snow; buses unable to run and trains held up for long periods while fresh falls were cleared from the line between the mountain passes.

Leading Wren Isabella Mackenzie was on leave pending demob. which meant she wouldn't have to return to her station ever again, but without civilian clothes she still wore uniform and now sat huddled in her greatcoat wishing the cabin heater would do a bit better. But she didn't really mind the cold for she was going home. Home to the castle which was, or would be in a few weeks, her own. Her mother had been captured by the Gestapo, taken to Fresnes prison and tortured and had finally died of rheumatic fever in the prison hospital.

Conversation was impossible in the noisy plane even if the pilot had not been in constant touch with Evanton by radio. Once or twice he glanced at his passenger sitting quietly, absorbed in her thoughts.

"Stuck-up," he decided; "looking down that long nose of hers. *And* no beauty either." With unlimited experience in such matters, he decided there would be no point in furthering the acquaintance. Even if he got beyond that ugly coat all he'd find would be a cross between scaffolding and a clothes horse. Not a cosy type at all. She caught his glance and smiled primly and distantly back.

The Moray Firth lay beneath them, a welcome break in the interminable expanse of white and he forgot Isabella as he went over in his mind the landing drill. There was only one runway on the little airfield - itself the only one operational in the north of Scotland, and his mind needed to be wholly concentrated on the Oxford's unendearing peculiarities, of which it had more than an acceptable share. It handled like a drunken rhinoceros he thought, as he hauled the heavy, sluggish machine round on the first circuit. It required enormous strength to keep it on course and he knew he would be in constant danger of stalling as its speed fell off and it began to lose height. One of its least attractive idiosyncrasies, and which made it such a dicey job to land, was this habit of stalling at a speed only fractionally lower than its maximum airspeed. Landing on that runway, cleared of snow but with black ice a certainty ...

The green winking light from the control tower showing it was clear to land, he brought the plane up into the wind, put the nose down with great care and, his eyes glued to the needles, began the long, slow glide down.

Five thousand; three; two; one. The needles fell rapidly on both altimeter and speed dial. He synchronised them as best he could (they could never be relied upon for complete accuracy) until he was quite sure he was going to make it first time. A tricky moment, this. If the approach was not perfectly judged; if either speed or height were wrong; if anything at all was misjudged; it could be too late to pull out of the glide to make another attempt and that would be very much that.

Five hundred feet and dropping fast. He levelled out as the speed came down and holding the plane steady with all his young strength did the best landing he could manage - not a complete belly flop but with the tail a fraction too high so the plane nearly tipped onto its nose. The Oxford skidded on the icy runway, slewed; was yanked back on course; held steady and they were safe, taxi-ing back to the collection of assorted huts which constituted the station's control offices.

Isabella stayed three nights with the Stewarts; just long enough for the chimneys in the West Wing to be swept and for a load of wood to be installed in a pantry at the foot of the backstairs. Then she moved into the castle.

The flat in the West Wing, being relatively small both in size of rooms and number, was slightly more snug than the rest of the house. Facing east over the courtyard it was also more or less sunless in winter. It had no view (in spite of its name) but there were compensations, as Isabella discovered. Rows of bookshelves in the sitting-room; a large fireplace and a tigerskin rug to lie on in front of the fire in the evenings. The flat had been occupied sporadically, but there had been no one since her mother's last visit there after the divorce, the various visitors to the estate, consisting mostly of Trustees, understandably preferring to lodge at the hotel in the village. But it was perfectly habitable with a small kitchen built into a cupboard; a cold tap, no bathroom but after a long walk across to the rest of the house, *the* lavatory, an impressive affair of blue willow-pattern china set in a stretch of gleaming mahogany as big as a table with a brass handle set into it. Well worth the walk through icy corridors. After two years in the Wrens comfort was not important.

But she didn't like her bedroom. This had no view at all except walls. The bed was hard, short and narrow, rather like the bunks with their thin straw palliasses in the hut she had shared with thirty-five other Wrens. There was a small electric fire with one bar that worked only when there were no power cuts, which was rare.

She did not mind the cold. It had been very cold at her station when the new Tummel-Garry hydro-electric scheme would not work as the reservoir was frozen over. A big oak chest in the hall had produced a bearskin rug along with other unidentifiable furry coverings, her great-uncle's coronation vestments or peer's robe and a moth-eaten plaid. The bearskin rug she put on her bed. The plaid she took upstairs and, during the next few weeks, when she wasn't playing the magnificent Bechstein piano in the dining-room, wandered with it wrapped round her over her own tartan skirt, fair-isle wool jersey and cardigan to match (knitted for her by Alison) through vast, dank, musty-smelling rooms. Mice scuttled behind the wainscotting, death-watch beetle heaped the floors with dust, and here and there a hole in the skirting-board looked too large, surely, to have been made by the mice. The place smelt: of decay, wet plaster and, overall, dry-rot. Not that she cared. It was home - and it was hers.

The snow continued, piling up against the drifts, so that walking, except where it had been cleared, was impossible. But she didn't mind. Each day was a delight, a revelation. There would be new places to explore; cupboards to open; chests to investigate. She lived through those days bewitched ... enchanted; with the treasures stacked in the drawing-room, dining-room, library, sitting-rooms, studies, morning-room, parlour. With the books which covered the walls of the library from floor almost to ceiling; pictures ... especially the pictures. Especially the family ones and, singled-out, the one of her namesake, Isabella, born Mackenzie, wife of the third Earl.

Looking at it one morning she was reminded of her first day at the castle when Angus had showed her round. Wandering round the room she had come to a halt beneath it, unable, because the picture was too dirty, to read the inscription. She had looked across to where the factor stood gloomily surveying a large damp patch above a window.

"Mr. Stewart," she called. "Who's this?"

He came to stand beside her.

"That's Isabella; wife to the third Earl. She'd be several times great-grandmother to ye." He turned to look at her. "Ay, and ye're like to each other. Ye've the same bonny hair and ye'll no be offendit if I tell ye Her Ladyship's nose is nae unlike yer ain."

"That's certainly no compliment," she retorted. Already she was losing her shyness with Angus and fast becoming as fond of him as she was of his wife. She trusted him and, had she been the most beautiful girl in Scotland, the manner of this excellent man towards the girl he looked upon as a sacred charge would have been exactly the same.

"Is that so? I like it well enough," he answered. He looked back at the picture. "Ay, she's a striking handsome wumman and she was a guid landlord in the Errl's absence, but for a' that she was wicked."

"Why? What did she do?"

"Well, there was a seer at the time - some 'yin who'll predict the future - what the Highlanders call the second sight - and he tauld the lady something she didna' care to hear."

"Oh?"

"Ay. The Errl was fra hame at the French Court in Parrus and she was wishful tae know what he was daein' and when he'd be coming back and sic ... her not having had nae word frae him long whiles."

"What happened?" asked Isabella.

"Och well, it seems the seer tauld her he'd 'seen' wi' his wee stane - some pebble he'd pickit up fra the beach in Lewis and had had since a bairn and had polished it and it had made him see things he couldna' 'a seen wi'out. And he tells Her

Ladyship that he'd 'seen' the Errl and he was fine and carousing wi' French lassies the whiles ... "

"What happened?" she asked again.

"Well, she was nae best pleased tae hear a' this and for a' she'd made the seer tell when he hadn'a wantit to she said he was a sorcerer and she'd have him burnt at the stake."

"And did she?"

"Nay. But she had him thrown intil a spiked barrel of burning tar. And the laird was e'en then on his way hame. He hairrd the news and he rode like a madman thinking to save the seer, until his horse deid beneath him, the puir beastie, when he was nearly at the spot and he rinned the last half mile to try and save the Seer."

"And did he?"

"Nay. He was too late."

"What a horrible woman she must have been," she said slowly. "And does the ghost of the seer haunt the castle?"

"There's nae ghosties here," had been Angus' decisive answer.

Thinking of this conversation, Isabella pulled forward a chair and climbed onto it and as the sky cleared, a pale shaft of sun fell across the portrait. It showed the wife of the third Earl as a striking woman indeed, but far from being a beauty. Indeed, the girl thought, she was really rather ugly, but mesmerisingly attractive. A face to hold the attention. Strong and rather masculine, and as little like the simpering beauties in their court dresses on either side of her as a hawk is like to songbirds. That strange, long nose so like Isabella's own ... Her dress was beautiful, thought the girl; of silver and mulberry satin. Huge pearls hung from her ears, round her neck and from a silver brooch at her bosom. The portrait shows her standing, one hand supporting a nosegay, the other lying still on her skirt.

"Perhaps her eyes are rather mocking ... they're very like mine as well as her nose ... but it's easy to imagine things in this place," she told herself.

She got down from the chair, walked rather impatiently across the floor towards the windows and sat down at the bureau between them. After a moment, and not without a slight feeling of guilt, she started opening drawers, for something to do; not because she was expecting to find anything. The bureau was a singularly beautiful piece of furniture: very tall, ornately decorated with graceful, curving wings which soared as though to meet each other in the middle, forming themselves at their apex into small, tightly-curled scrolls. Some of the drawers looked as though they should open and didn't; some did and were empty. Yet others were let into the bow-shaped side of the bureau and moved sideways a little, turning half back to front before she could see into them. Twiddling, feeling and pressing - removing drawers wherever she could, she came finally upon a long, curved secret one, reaching far to the back and presenting a blank front to a careless observer. In it was a small leather-bound book with silver clasps.

With a slightly worried glance at the portrait of her ancestress (was it her fancy that the eyes were upon her? Of course: What else?) she undid the clasps and opened the little book, half expecting poetry or sayings or even sermons. But all the yellowing pages with their irregular brown stained edges were blank. There was nothing in it to connect it with its owner. She went half through it, turning the pages carelessly in twos and threes - not bothering to separate the leaves which clung damply together. As she turned it over, a piece of folded paper fell out onto the bureau. It too was damp, yellow and mouldy, but it had writing on it. She got up and went to sit on a window seat. She unfolded it and began to read:-

34

<u>Extract from the journal of Isobel Seafort</u>:

<u>The Burning</u>

'I stand watching them, the Black Priest at his curious antics, the Raven at his. One is behaving like a madman, pressing something to his eye, holding it up towards a single black candle, prostrating himself over and over again. The other - the Raven - is pecking at the remains of food - some peasant's leavings - near the fire. They look much like each other; both making pecking and skipping gestures. But the one fills me with contempt and loathing, though I fear him too, while the other ... the Raven ... is an omen of ill. It is too close to me; it fills me with foreboding. I frighten it away but it returns. And if it were to do that - to return - He said, then should I look to my soul. But I care nothing for these warnings; my soul has been in the Devil's keeping since that accursed day. The day of the Feast. And the Prophecy.

The Black Priest is still at his satanic devotions. Would that he put an end to them. I am weary of this capering, prating, treacherous cleric and his demonic ravings. He has served his purpose and claimed two souls for his own. Now would that he were gone, like the Other, where he will trouble me no more. I wish him dead, but to die without the screams and the agony. My God, those screams. They will go with me into my grave.

I look across the Ness. The Black Priest suddenly raises his arm and throws a stone ... *The* stone. The Seer's, not that prating fool's. He throws it with all the strength of his arm away towards the sea. He turns, raises his hand in farewell to me and walks towards the

35

castle. (So it did not work for him then, for all his unpriestly antics!) I wait until he has shut the door. Then I go to the edge of the sea and it is there - such an ordinary-looking little blue-white stone - for all that it is the shape of an elfin moon; for all that it has in its power to change my destiny and that of my descendants, and, for all I know, the destiny of countless others. But I must hasten. The wind has got up and the waves are bigger. I bend swiftly and before the long arm of the next one can claw it from the strand to bury it beneath itself, I have it in my hand. My stone now. And perhaps mine the power to undo the terrible harm caused by its misuse in the hands of the Seer. For me, now, to redress the evil and turn it into good. But my own act of evil can never be redressed for I sent him to his death, for all that I did so unwittingly. Not even the Stone can give him new life now, nor still the screams that ring forever in my ears.'

The clock on the mantelpiece whirred and shook itself, preparing to strike. Isabella leapt up. Everyday she had lunch with the Stewarts and today she was going to be late. She'd have to run all the way.

The great banks of dirty snow began to melt at last and with the thaw came the snowdrops and then the daffodils known locally as 'lilies'; hundreds of clumps of them, many-layered within; green rather than yellow, and smelling of scented earth. Alison called them witchen but Isabella, though inclined to agree with her (for they were totally unlike the artificial-looking things which appeared decorously just as they were planted and had no smell in Aunt Kitty's prim Surrey garden) loved them. For their strange appearance, their smell and the way they scattered themselves, wandering as far as they could go as the garden turned into fields. Often the sun shone now with some warmth and it was on one of those sunny days that Isabella decided to change her room. Perhaps she was prompted by the portrait, liking the idea of sleeping in her ancestress's room. Angus had told her the castle had been completely changed and reorganised during the reign of James I. Perhaps it was a challenge her adventurous spirit could not resist (for it *could* be haunted, whatever Angus said). Whatever the reason and after a morning spent in the linen room trying to find a pair of sheets she wouldn't immediately put her feet through) she at last assembled a collection of cold and slippery linen sheets and pillowcases most beautifully embroidered and monogrammed; lugged them down several passages together with two square pillows and hairy blankets, stiff with much washing, and paused at the door of her new room.

She opened the door, letting her burden slide to the floor and at that moment the room was full of sun. It was huge and faced south over the verandah and as she stared, entranced, the shafts of sunlight with their swimming motes played over the ancient cobwebs which festooned the indigo-blue velvet curtains and their tarnished gold-trimmed pelmets. She stood looking, as though she had happened on a discovery for she had never before seen the room with the sun in it, while the sunlight cast beams of untarnished gold over her feet.

She made the bed, noticing properly for the first time its twisted gilded posts and interleavings and the splendidly decorated gold satin counterpane and furnishings. It was a massive affair of some antiquity since it was very wormy and the paint was flaking away. It was also exceedingly hard, though comfortable enough as she discovered when her labours were completed and she lay back in the sunshine, her legs spread, curling and uncurling her toes; thinking deeply; aware of a strange feeling of anticipation - of being a small step closer to whatever it was she had to do. For there was something. She hadn't entirely imagined the expression on the Countess's face; the warning look ... not warning exactly, but from then on, whenever she looked at the portrait she thought she detected a new expression. Perhaps not warning; perhaps urgency ...'and perhaps I'm just being ridiculous and imaging things' thought the young Isabella, as she'd thought so often before. But she couldn't put it from her mind, nor did she feel she was meant to. Not the look, nor the page with its jagged inside edge so obviously torn from a journal, so nobody would see it. Burning; the Stone; Him (meaning the Seer). The Countess's own part in it. (Well, everyone knew that.) All fitted in with the story Angus had told her. The only thing that didn't fit was the Stone itself ... and Isabella's character. True she looked to be both haughty and strong-minded. Perhaps even sometimes harsh. But the face the girl saw every day did not fit in with the sentiments on the page torn from the journal. Here she talked of her own 'act of evil' and of the 'redress of evil' and, still more worryingly, 'mine the power to undo the terrible harm caused by its misuse at the hands of the Seer'. 'Its misuse' ... meaning obviously the Stone. But the legendary stone had not resembled an elfin moon. It had been what Angus called 'cam' or blind, 'one-eyed' ... with a hole in the middle (hence the term often applied to one who has the second sight as possessing a third eye). Nor had it been as she described it. It was supposed to have been black and the Seer had thrown it away - into a cow's hoofprint and water had welled up through the hole, spreading and spreading until it had formed a big loch.

Perhaps not so horrible after all - the Countess. Perhaps the Seer had deserved his fate.

THE STONE

The fearsome winter was followed by a hot golden summer and Isabella blossomed. She put on weight and for the first time in her life she knew what it was to be happy. Happy or contented. Perhaps the latter is best because it is less evanescent. Even the malign, formerly three-weekly flood now remained within bounds and its allotted timespan, and she had no hesitation in attributing this alleviation of her hated burden to the beneficial influence of the Stone. With it had come a purpose to her life and though she still didn't know what it was she had to do, she was indeed content.

Every day that she could, while the heatwave lasted, she swam in the river in a deep brown pool, so dark it looked black. The fishing was let and the boat, tied to an alder tree by a long chain just below the river walk, was her great blessing, for the bank was far too steep for her to climb out again. The water, swift-flowing and fed by the many burns which had tumbled in spate down the steep sides of many scored hills was icy cold except for the top layer which was warm and felt like brown silk. Here she swam or lay in the boat in the sun, half asleep; dreaming.

On other days she would walk up the hill behind the castle to the Black Rock which towered over it, continuing on up the rock until she came to the loch which lay to the north-east and was called Loch Ussie because of the legend of the Seer's stone. The other, legendary stone? Perhaps. She would sit on a crumbling log covered with scratchy grey litchen, her bare feet squelching delightfully in the cool wet, bright green sphagnum moss. Amongst the moss and the bog cotton and the bog myrtle, which smelt so fragrant when crushed, Isabella sat and thought of the two Stones and her part in whatever it was and gazed at the dark, still water of the loch. As a believer gazes avidly all day upon the waters of Loch Ness hoping for a glimpse of the Monster, so did she gaze at her own loch of legend, hoping that the kelpie - the 'each uisge', or water horse also of legend, who she was certain dwelt there, would rise up and confront her, a pair of human lungs in his jaws. Or perhaps he would come up out of the loch, an irresistible, perfect little horse and invite her to climb on his back, whereupon he would rush with her into the loch, carrying her down, down to his watery stable far below the surface; and next day it would be her own lungs which he would have in his jaws when he surfaced for fresh prey.

'Whatever will Alison say when they tell her I've been eaten by the water horse of Loch Ussie?' she thought, laughter bubbling up in her.

Her twenty-first birthday came and went unmarked externally save for a telegram from Aunt Kitty and family and a letter from her Senior Trustee, telling her he was now authorised to hand over 'monies' in the form of a capital sum of £25,000. Although this was still to be held in trust, it was invested so as to produce a greatly increased income over her present allowance of £150 a year. Isabella was unimpressed. She had few expenses; the Estate saw to all that and there was nothing to buy anyway in Britain in 1947. But she remembered that birthday for two things: the jersey which Alison had knitted for her and the supreme sacrifice of their combined sweet and sugar rations to make a chocolate cake with twenty-one pink candles which Alison 'had by'. They promised a party for her later, before the harvest, to meet her tenants, which would be held not - alas - in the castle itself, because the big rooms were still crammed with furniture from the military occupation, but in one of the Nissen huts where there were trestle tables.

This, when it happened, was something she would never forget. Alison had prepared a spread such as even Scottish farmers were no longer accustomed to. They drank her health; the men in thimble-sized glasses of whisky; the women in strong tea. They presented her with a little gold watch, inscribed with her initials, which she put on immediately. She thanked them all shyly and (prewarned by Angus) said she hoped very much that they would all get to know each other better and how happy she was to have come among them. Mrs. Macdonald gave her verdict later sitting with Mrs. Duncan over black tea in the kitchen at home. 'A bonny enough lassie wi' nice manners. Too thin; bonny hairr; time she was married but she'll do,' was the general opinion among the women, who were prepared to like her.

The men who had eyed her covertly as she bounded up and down the hut to the tune of Lady Isabella's Feast played on the pipes were secretly disappointed at her total lack of sex appeal, or indeed any comely curves beneath the severe, long-sleeved, high-fastening grey dress with its demure white collar upon which their lustful eyes could rest. Mrs. Duncan's husband, notable for his propensity for wandering, and whose eyes had rested upon Isabella's immature chest a trifle overlong in spite of everything, on catching his wife's terrible look, could only be thankful that here at least there was no temptation.

Alison wasn't quite so sure. Tonight, the girl was noticed; made to feel herself wanted and important; enjoying herself as she had never done before. She was wearing a glow of something very like radiance, which lit up her normally plain features which could sometimes be so ugly, and brought a becoming pink flush to her high cheekbones. And she *was* enjoying herself, thought Alison, who had been greatly worried

41

by the girl's odd, lonely ways. If she could but find herself a husband ... a proper one who'd help her with the estate. 'It's too much of a burden for a lassie,' she thought. Her look, falling at that moment upon Isabella's current partner, made her shake her head.

"Ay," said Angus at her side; "he's awa' a'ready wi' his cozening ways. But he's no for her ... not Kenneth Mackenzie ... for a' that it'd suit him fine."

"Who was that?" asked Isabella at lunch next day.

"Och, ye'll be meaning Kenneth Mackenzie, wha' danced yer ain reel wi' ye. He's just anither of them; there's a wheen Mackenzies here ye ken."

"Why is he called Kenneth Mackenzie? He speaks like an Englishman," asked Isabella.

"Maybe he's been educatit down south," replied Angus. "I dinna ken. He's one of the tenants. It's mostly the sheep he does best wi'."

"Did you like him, dearie?" asked Alison rather anxiously.

"Not much," confessed Isabella. "I didn't like his eyes, and considering I'd never met him before, he was awfully familiar. He asked me to come to see him."

"And what did ye say?" enquired Angus, trying not to sound worried.

"I said I might; that's all. Why, don't you like him either?"

"It's nae that. But it wudn'a do for ye to have him thinking he can ... weel, ye're the laird, Miss Isabella, and ye'll no mind my saying that a bit lassie with a grreat inheritance like yer ain wud be a temptation tae any man howmsoever he is seetuated and worrthy to tak' ye for wife."

"Oh, it's not like that," said Isabella. "Nobody ever wants to even get to know me better, let alone marry me, in spite of my inheritance. At least nobody has yet."

"Perhaps they didn'a ken aboot it," said Angus drily.

"Anyway, I'm much too plain and ... well, men don't like me. Anymore than I like them," she added defiantly.

Alison looked at her with pity.

"Ye'll find someone one day who will, my bairn," she said reassuringly. "And we must hope the day comes soon for you'll need someone to help you run this big place ... in the meanwhile, there's no doubt that it would be best to keep away from Kenneth."

"Why, what's he done?"

Angus leant forward and spoke very seriously.

"See ye here, Miss Isabella. Alison and I are as fond of ye as if ye were our ain bairn, which we sair wish we'd been able to have, and it wud nae be richt, nae mair than we'd be doing our duty towards ye if we didn'a warrn ye of yon. He got a lassie into trouble ... aye, and refused to acknowledge the bairn. And he's ower fond of the bottle; not that that wud matter if ... "

"If what, Mr. Stewart?"

"Well, it's ither trouble besides lassies he's been in," said Angus reluctantly. He glanced at his wife. "It's trouble with the Polus ... for cruelty to animals. He takes a drap too much whiles and then ... It seems Donny the Post, ca' upon him one afternoon wi' a telegram and heard terrible noises like as though a cat was being tortured. He tauld the Polus and they paid him a wheen visits and they found a' sorts of things they shouldn'a."

Isabella would have liked to ask what, but kept quiet.

"He was prosecutit and fined £5 and given a warrning. But it seems that ... well, it's no' just the drink and the cruelty but a bit mair else."

Here Alison shook her head slightly and made as if to intervene.

"Nay, Alison. The lassie must know it a' ... then she can

43

mak' up her ain mind and no say we didn'a tell her."

"I wouldn't ever," declared Isabella indignantly.

"And fine I ken it," he replied warmly. "Anyways, it was Mrs. Macdonald from the East Lodge ... she went awa' up the Rock tae veesit her sister and on the way back she says she saw lichts and they were blue and sort of waving aboot and she heard the same kind of noises as Donny, as of an animal being tortured."

"That auld witch," exclaimed Alison scornfully. "It surprises me she hasna' yet seen the Devil himself. And what would a body be wanting wi' blue lichts of an evening, I'd like to know?"

"There's talk of that too," said her husband grimly. "Sacrificing animals to the Devil in some wicked rite or ither. But there's nae denying yon's a queer body. I'd like fine to be rid of him."

"Can't you have him ... er ... evicted?" asked Isabella without any clear idea of what it meant.

"Ay; but it wud be verra deeficult to find anither tenant. The land's nae guid - it's a' rock and there's sae little soil cover it's only guid for the sheep. And he pays his rent on time. You see, Miss Isabella the estate needs a' the rent it can get to cover the costs and the tax and a'. And guid tenants dinna grow on trees. We'll let him bide sae lang as he behaves himself, and I ken fine ye'll no let us a' doon by giving him ony excuse not tae. We count on ye."

Isabella promised and went away in a thoughtful mood. To a girl of her spirit Angus and Alison's warnings could have had the opposite to the desired effect, but the charge of cruelty to animals made her think. Anyway she hadn't liked the young man; in fact he had repelled her and even slightly alarmed her when at one moment during the reel they had come face to face and she had looked up to see his slightly unpleasant,

44

calculating eyes on her.

That afternoon all thoughts of Kenneth Mackenzie went straight out of her head. In the same drawer as she had found the little leather journal (which she had not opened since returning it to its hiding place in some haste), at the very back, as her fingers scrabbled to get a hold on the journal, they closed instead on The Stone.

It lay in her hand; polished to an almost glassy smoothness, marble-white - and the shape of an elfin moon.

It lay there for a long time, Isabella staring at it, occasionally feeling it gingerly, wondering, wondering, her brain a whirling mass of questions.

This was it then, the Seer's stone; this was the true one of the Prophecies. The black 'cam' stone through which water oozed and after which the loch was called, was the legendary one. This was the Stone that the Countess had seen thrown into the waves and which she had rescued, hoping it could undo some of the harm it had already done. But, mused Isabella, staring at it in awe; surely it would not be capable of both; either it is a force for good or for evil; and how potent a force? And in whose hands? And what did you have to do with it, always supposing you were the right person to make it work its magic? Highland on both sides, all down the centuries, it would have been odd indeed if she hadn't inherited the Highland susceptibility to all kinds of superstitious fancies, but that she possessed the faculties of the 'taibhsear' or possessor the second sight she strongly doubted. Never in her life had she dreamt of portents or seen a ghost; in these last few months spent alone in the castle she had seen nothing and heard nothing other than the usual creakings and scratchings common to rodent-infested, uncared for old buildings. She felt she must be immune or just not psychic.

Cautiously she stroked the Stone wondering if, like Aladdin's brass lamp, a genie would suddenly appear to grant her every wish. Almost fearfully she waited, glancing round the room as if he were already there, a tiny green figure like a leprechaun, wearing a silly hat, perched, grinning, on top of the Countess's portrait.

Isabella put the Stone down on the desk and with the loss of contact came an extraordinary feeling - of profound desolation and an unpleasant sense of doom; of something dreadful which could be about to happen to her or to someone or to something. She picked up the Stone again and the feeling vanished. To repeat the little experiment would be a mistake, she felt. It would give her imagination an opportunity to take matters into its own hands. Once that had happened she might lose control over her powers, whatever they were, and probably over her destiny.

But she couldn't carry it in her hand all the time. She'd have to put it down sooner or later. This was ridiculous. She couldn't allow her life to be governed by a small white stone, whether it had magical properties or not. Yet had she any choice? She remained undecided for a few moments, still looking at where it lay in her hand, wondering, as well as what it could do for her (if indeed she wanted it to do anything at all), what effect it had had on the life of her ancestress, after she had rescued it from the waves on the day of The Burning. 'Was the Countess able to redress her wrongs?' wondered the girl. 'Did she make any prophesies, or did it not work for her? And what of all the Seer's unfulfilled prophesies? Could she, Isabella, carry on, three hundred years after the true Seer's death?' She looked again at the portrait. Again there seemed to be a strange look on the Countess's dark countenance.

Isabella wrapped the Stone in her handkerchief and tied

the corners round it. Then, because neither her skirt nor her jersey had pockets, she slipped it into her knickers, hoping the elastic would be strong enough to keep it there. She walked across the room and climbed up on the chair.

Now, as she stared, she seemed to sense a bond between them - the two Isabella Mackenzies. Up till now she hadn't been sure whether the Countess was a friend or an enemy; or if nothing quite so drastic, was she on her side or not? Now she knew. And she knew her own feelings. Whatever her ancestress had done; whatever wickedness she had committed, Isabella knew for certain, through the possession of the Stone, that though the Seer had possibly not deserved his fate, and was not necessarily the wicked one, the Countess was the one who had had to take the blame.

●

She went to bed early that night because she wanted to think about this extraordinary thing that had happened to her - her new find - now tucked under her pillow with her fingers curled round it. And as she thought and wondered, she must have slept, for she awoke, very much later with the moonlight on her face, to sounds all round her. Heavy footsteps, as of men wearing boots tramping past her door; carriage wheels splashing through puddles; voices everywhere; horses hooves clattering on the drive. And a great, roistering racket downstairs as though a feast was being held in the hall. For a few moments she lay in a dazed stupor, unbelieving of the strange clamour all round her; puzzled and a little afraid.

She heard the pipes playing and recognised the tune of 'The Lady Isabella's Feast', the reel which had been danced in her honour at her birthday party. It was impossible to mistake it. Impossible to mistake either the voice which, the reel ended, was being raised in a melancholy ballad; and so clear, in spite of the accompanying din, was this voice, that she could hear

47

the Gaelic words sung by the man she had danced her reel with
- Kenneth Mackenzie.

At this point she put her hand under the pillow feeling
for the Stone. Immediately she ceased to feel alarmed and
became extremely interested. But when she started to get out
of bed to investigate - if necessary to go downstairs, the whole
thing faded. There was no cessation of sound; it just became
fainter; then returned; retreated - each time becoming fainter
until it vanished.

The next day, only partly convinced that the whole thing
had been a dream, she went out half expecting to find traces of
the kind a number of carriages would leave. There would be
wheel-tracks surely, and horses' droppings; footprints; litter,
even. But there was nothing. Only yesterday's tracks made by
her bicycle and a few, older tyre marks made by the Vauxhall.
Nothing in the house either, though she looked carefully for
the sort of things she imagined might have been left by guests
from another century after a feast. Yes, but which century?
And Kenneth Mackenzie's voice was so clear ... so real. It was
disconcerting but interesting and a lot of questions needed
answering. If the whole thing hadn't been a dream then either
the castle or the room was haunted ... unless the Stone was
responsible. And if either or both were the case it ... in some
form ... would probably happen again.

Another thing that puzzled her, long after she had
recovered from the shock of what she'd heard that night, was
why she wasn't more afraid. Logically she should have either
changed her room or admitted defeat and gone to live with
Alison, who had never liked her being on her own in the castle.
But instead of intensified fear, it was curiosity which kept the
upper hand, though there were slight misgivings; but only
because she felt some situation might arise which would be

beyond her to deal with. But she had the Stone. Nothing could happen to her. And it was all intended, with more to come. Of that she was quite certain.

Nevertheless she decided on a bit of questioning. There were things ... aspects of the visitation upon which Angus might be able to throw light.

"How long were the military here for, Mr. Stewart?" she asked him one day at lunch.

"Nae ower lang; aboot six months."

"Did the soldiers camp in the park in tents, or in the house?"

"They were a' billeted in yon Nissen huts. And the officers were a' in the castle, as I tauld ye." (Was this a rebuke? Should she stop there?)

"Yes. I remember." She looked at him squarely. "Did ... I mean, were there lots of horses with the soldiers?"

"Nay, Miss Isabella. Naething like that. The Army doesna' use them nowadays. The only horses I kenned of in a' ma time here wud be the farrm yins. The sodgers a' had wee trucks and there were some of those new four-wheel drive things; jeeps. And verra useful they'd be for getting aboot the farms."

"Then ... ?" For a moment Isabella was tempted to ask why she'd heard horses, so many of them, in the park on that night, but until she was quite sure of what she was beginning to suspect ... that she was in some way connected (of course with the finding of the Stone), and being drawn back to the past - or at any rate being forced to communicate with it - she wanted to reveal as little as possible. It might worry them, her good friends. Instead she asked:

"Has the castle been occupied by the military at any other time in its history?"

"Ay, that it has. It was the headquarters of General Wade after the '45 Rising. Which is why it is as ye see it noo. There's

49

nae like the meelitary when it comes to a quick demolition job. They're awfu' destructive." He rose from the table and her opportunity was past.

That could be an explanation. Why and who in the past required her ... soul, obviously, since it could not have her person, was something that would probably reveal itself in time. She was still puzzled about the incident, but extraordinarily, at that time, had not for the moment wondered about the man she had heard.

In the meanwhile, she was getting on terms with the Stone. On the whole there wasn't much to it that she could discover. As long as it remained within her reach and did not lose contact with it for more than a moment or two, she was alright. Only once more had she experimented with putting it back in the dresser, but the feeling of doom and desolation and of some indescribable evil hovering near her returned with such force - far greater than the first time - that there must have been some warning that someone was trying to convey to her. But it could not have been responsible for the nocturnal incident - unless she had in her sleep felt under the pillow and touched it. That was quite possible. But as for it giving her powers to see into the future, no amount of stroking and handling it had yet done this. And it was a problem to know where to keep it. She tried hanging it round her neck in a bag suspended by a chord, but it showed through her jersey. So for the moment she kept it in her knickers; those highly serviceable, most unglamourous garments made of dark blue, thick cotton which had formed part of her uniform. They were not glamorous, but they were certainly warm.

KENNETH

It was now August and a good harvest was expected, though as is usual in that part of Scotland, it is a month later than in the south. In the few months that Isabella had been home she had shed much of her gawkiness and some of her shyness, replacing them with dignity and presence. She looked well and her curse still remained within its proper bounds (though it was odd that it always came with the new moon; the elfin moon which looked so like the Stone). She was finding her feet and beginning, at Angus' insistence, to take an interest in the daily running of the estate. He welcomed her presence and often took her with him when he went to visit the tenants and always to the town on market day. And he soon discovered that there was nothing contrived about her interest. She was born to be a laird even though not brought-up to it. But now she never forgot anything he told her; frequently she asked the sort of questions the trustees never bothered with, and she was beginning to come up with ideas for improvements in practically every aspect of estate management and animal husbandry. The only thing she seemed loath to learn about were accounts and for this Angus didn't blame her. Either one has a talent for them or one hasn't, in which case they are better left to the professionals, especially where the fearsomely complicated system of estate management is concerned.

She was popular with the tenants, already able to discuss crops and livestock in a knowledgeable manner. They liked her and respected her, and when the harvest started, being short of labour after the repatriation of Italian and German prisoners-of-war, their own lads being either no more to return, or still serving abroad, they gladly accepted her offer of help.

Her sleeves rolled up, she worked hard - sweatingly hard - under the hot sun and they liked it when from time to time she would wipe her brow with her long hair, before swinging another forkful up to the man in the hay wagon. Sometimes she drove the old horse at the Home Farm who pulled the reaper or drove the pre-war tractor (Angus had already taught her how to drive the Vauxhall) which broke down often and could not be used where the land was steep or boggy. The women liked her because she made no attempt to distract their menfolk and they were all ready to a woman for any signs of incipient flirtation. But Isabella had worked among sailors for two years and this now stood her well ... especially when on market days, discussing stock with Angus, her elbows on the pens, she received many curious looks at the odd sight of a girl in her position and of her age playing at being a farmer.

On Sundays - this time at Alison's insistence - she went with them to church, neat in her grey dress and a black velvet beret with her caberfeidh (stag's head) brooch pinned to it. It bored her but with Scotland in those days being both God-fearing and feudal, it would have been unthinkable for her not to attend. It was attired in this highly suitable outfit that she was persuaded to have lunch at the local hotel with her Senior Trustee who, alarmed at reports from neighbours which had filtered through to him via acquaintances, considered it high time he came to see for himself the whole set-up - Isabella living alone in the castle; Isabella attending livestock sales; Isabella helping with the hay harvest ...

Too busy; too taken up with her new life, she had reckoned without neighbours. One or two did call but without success, as the doorbell had not worked for years and a brisk tug would cause the rusty handle to fall out of its socket followed by long coils of equally rusty wire. Or she was out; or watching behind the drawing-room curtains, longing for them to go away. Eventually the neighbours must have come to a decision not to waste precious petrol and tyres on someone who was never there and didn't return the calls of those who presented their cards to Alison at the Estate Office. But their factors knew Angus and in the bar of the pub, where he took Isabella to lunch each Wednesday, he told them as much about her as he saw fit. Thus she was able to avoid them.

But she couldn't avoid the Wotherspoons - father and son - who were waiting for her in the lounge as Angus drove her up to the hotel entrance, and with his usual courtesy got out and opened the door for her.

Mr. Wotherspoon was a cousin of her mother's, the head of an important firm of Writers to the Signet in Edinburgh. Over the years his firm had greatly profited, as such firms will, from absentee landlords and the volume of business which the estate had brought in and this one was highly profitable. A self-consequent man of little personal charm, he typified the family lawyer, but he was efficient and possessed of a conscience. This had been slightly troubling him of late. Isabella's position was the cause and it was time something was done about the girl. It was alright while she had remained in her aunt's care or was still in the Wrens. But she had been virtually on her own (he didn't count the Stewarts) for six months, living in the castle. Alone. Most unsuitable for a girl of only twenty-one. It was time, yes it was certainly time, she was taken in hand. She must meet he right sort of young men, for the sooner she was married the better. Stewart was a good agent, he had to acknowledge, and had run the estate competently for a long time, but the war had changed things so. Ideas, methods, machinery. All must be brought up to date. That Isabella neither wanted nor needed a husband didn't occur to him, and even if it had, he would not have believed it. All women needed a man behind them. A guiding hand and some sort of control, 'otherwise heaven knows what she'll take it into her head to do,' he thought ... remembering with a shudder Isabella's mother's goings-on. So it was with the amiable intention of making her an offer to pay them an indefinite visit, as well as some business, that he was here today. And he had brought with him his son.

They rose from the sofa in the hotel lounge and took a step towards her as she came through the door, Angus having dropped her off on his way to the town. She took off her beret as she entered and ran her fingers through her hair. They paused, somewhat disconcerted to find that she at least half a head taller than either of them. In spite of their smiles, Isabella, practised in discernment, knew already that they did not like her. Ronald Wotherspoon, a spotty young man only three years older than she was, but very much older in vice and avarice, was thinking as he stood lumpishly before her, fingering one of his spots, something along the same lines as the Oxford's pilot. Now there was more of Isabella visible and he didn't think he liked any of it. However there was no denying that she *was* an heiress; he rather fancied himself as laird, even though it was all falling to bits. Once he'd hooked her, he thought vulgarly, he could get on with his own inclinations. Also, as he well knew, there was a good deal of money attached to this set-up - something like ten thousand fertile acres of land; fishing (some of the finest in Scotland); shooting and what-have-you. 'Once the Trust comes to an end,' he thought, 'when she's twenty-five or married, then there's nothing to stop me from selling off bits here and there.' A house in the South of France would be alright; a Rolls Royce - no, a Jaguar would be more his style; a yacht; a flat in London. Unconsciously he began rubbing his hands together, ceasing abruptly as his father's gaze fell upon him. However, he was not going to be frowned-down by his father; made to look a fool before this girl. But my God, she's

54

ugly! Just like that picture of some ancestress or other that he'd seen on his only visit to the castle. That's another thing, he thought: pictures. A Lawrence; Allan Ramsay; Benjamin West; and best of all, Raeburn. There'd be a market for those before long. Oh yes, no shortage of money there.

Lunch was not a success. Mr. Wotherspoon, at his most persuasive, pointed out all the advantages of a prolonged sojourn in Edinburgh. He pulled out all the stops. He talked of clothes, of theatres and concerts, of parties and visits to London. He unfolded what seemed to him to be a glorious vista of opportunity before her, while his son stuffed himself noisily with food. But it was of no use. At the end of it all Isabella merely thanked him and said that she was rather busy at the moment helping with the haymaking.

"But my dear child," expostulated Mr. Wotherspoon, "that's not a job for a girl. Surely there are plenty of men? After the haymaking, then?" After the haymaking came the harvest, explained Isabella patiently, and as though to an imbecile.

"Well, then," said Mr. Wotherspoon querulously. He was both baffled and exasperated by her lack of enthusiasm, bordering, he thought, on rudeness. "After that?"

"Thank you very much. It's very kind of you to ask me, but I don't like parties and clothes and things like that. I'd rather stay here and help Mr. Stewart."

"Don't be ridiculous," said Mr. Wotherspoon sharply. "How can you help him. You're not legally entitled to make any decisions concerning the estate until you are either twenty-five years old or married." And it's going to be a job to pull that off if she doesn't take to Ronald, he thought, intercepting Isabella's scornful glance at his son. It was obvious already that there was little chance of anything of the sort.

"Oh, I don't do anything like that. I only go with him to

55

see the tenants and talk to them and to the market so I can learn about stock. And he's teaching me to drive as well," she added rather naively.

However much the lawyer thought she'd be far better off with Mrs. Stewart learning all the home skills which, in his view, were all women needed to know, he could not get away from the fact that it was her estate. There was a strong possibility that she might not take to Ronald, or indeed anyone else, and remaining permanently unmarried, and also as she was obviously no fool (in spite of his dislike he had to admit that) when she came of age she might remove her business from him and take it elsewhere. He thought of large sums of money making their way into a rival firm's pockets and was dismayed. If only Ronnie were older; taller; more attractive to women - the right sort of women. If only he wasn't such an oaf, thought his devoted father, watching sauce ooze out of the corner of his son's mouth and slither slowly down his spotty chin, something might yet come of it.

He never discovered that Ronnie, a few weeks later, had given both his parents the slip and had journeyed north with the intention (as he thought of it with his usual lack of finesse) of 'having a go' at Isabella.

He got no further than the station, neatly frustrated by Angus who was collecting some spare parts for the tractor off the train from Inverness. Much to his annoyance (the cheek of this factor person; didn't he know who he was?) he found himself marched smartly off to lunch at the hotel, returned to the station and put on the train back to Inverness.

"Miss Isabella's no seeing visitors;" Angus had told him, "she's helping wi' the harrvest. There's no saying if she's wishfu' to see ye, and if ye are mindit for it, it's nae mair nor five miles. I'm sorry I canna' tak ye there, but I maun bide for a worrd wi' the bank manager."

It was a hot day with biting flies and clouds of bloodthirsty midges. Ronnie, no walker, decided on a graceful retreat, especially if Isabella was going to treat him in the same manner as this upstart employee, now looking at him thoughtfully but with a twinkle in his blue eyes and an amused grin lurking at the corners of his mouth.

Lunch finished, refusing coffee, Isabella rose to go. She would walk home, she said. Ignoring further expostulations she hurried from the room and once clear of the hotel, she ran till well out of sight. "One more second I'd have been so rude to him," she thought with a sigh. "Oh well. And that disgusting boy!"

She slowed to a walk before the big gates and was just about to leave the road for the drive when a car drew up behind her and stopped. She turned and out of the battered Commer van stepped Kenneth Mackenzie.

"Hello," he said. "It's quite a long time since we met. Do you remember dancing Lady Isabella's Feast with me at your party Miss Mackenzie?"

"Oh yes. Of course I do. You're Kenneth Mackenzie. One of my tenants," she added, determined to keep this somewhat upstart young man firmly in his place. She was immediately sorry. It was a vulgar thing to say and had somehow put her at a disadvantage. But he seemed rather amused.

"As you say. One of your tenants. I'm on my way home. May I give you a lift? Save you the long walk up the drive to your ancestral pile." He was looking at her, still with amusement, but there was speculation, or something she didn't much care for as well. Nor did she like his eyes, any more than she had the first time they met. She would have liked to refuse but did not want to be rude again or appear stand-offish.

"Alright," she said with dignity. "Thanks."

In the car conversation was almost impossible, as it had been in the Oxford, such was the noise made by the disintegrating vehicle as it leapt the ruts and fell into pot-holes. Isabella clutching at the door as her seat slid back and forth, was trying to think of something to say. It wouldn't after all be polite to remain in total silence for the whole of the four-mile trip and she was just about to utter some inane remark about the weather, when the young man beside her suddenly began to sing, which brought her bolt upright, her mouth wide open in shock, for not only had she heard that song before, but she was sitting beside the person who had sung it ... the ballad she had heard that night not so very long ago. She was still trying to assimilate the fact (this was fact and no dream) when as if to confirm it - the strangeness of this person, her tenant, and as they approached the North Lodge - a dog suddenly darted out of a field in front of the car.

"Look out you bloody animal," he shouted and the car gave a violent swerve, almost precipitating both Isabella and her seat into his lap.

"Sorry about that," he said easily. "I wish to God those people would keep that dog under control. This is the second time I've nearly run the damned thing over."

But Isabella wasn't listening. She had seen his face and was for a brief second horribly frightened. Her one thought was to make him stop and let her get out before they got to the North Lodge. The last thing she wanted after the Stewarts' warning was for them to see her in Mackenzie's company. Perhaps they would not immediately see any harm in him giving her a lift most of the way home; indeed it would have been very odd if he hadn't, but they had warned her against him in no uncertain manner and the instinct for self-preservation was very strong. Also she was no fool, she was growing up rapidly and instinct told her quite simply and unequivocably that the less she had to do with this ... this 'taibh' or spectre the better. But what *was* he really? What was this all about? One thing she did know was that she was going to heed that warning.

"Stop here, please. I'll walk home." It sounded curt, patronising again. "I need some exercise after all that lunch," she said hurriedly, trying to laugh. But glancing at him, she thought she saw a flash of anger in the light, unpleasant eyes.

"I can easily run you to the castle," he said rather coldly. "It's no trouble."

Why was he so anxious for her company, she wondered. She'd never given him the slightest encouragement - in fact she'd always been rather rude.

"No thanks, really. I'd like to walk. I've been shut up in the hotel for two hours having lunch with my awful trustee and his even awfuller son. Don't turn in at the gates ... if you'd just stop here ... "

He pulled up and reached out his arm across her to open the door but she forestalled him, shoved it open, leapt out and with a quick wave had gone. It wasn't until she had nearly reached the castle that a thought occurred to her. The car hadn't swerved to *avoid* the dog. Kenneth Mackenzie had deliberately tried to run it over. "He can't have," she said aloud. "He wouldn't do a thing like that, however bad he is." But even as she spoke she knew she was right.

To arrive at an understanding of supernatural or occult happenings, seeings, visitations, it is necessary to consult, not the self-designated experts - accredited 'taibhsears' (those supposedly of the second sight), soothsayers, mediums, crystal balls, lumps of lead in boiling water, tea leaves ... the whole bag of charlatanic tricks, but the clear-sighted (and headed) serious researchers into the subject. These people approach the matter scientifically and this is the only way. Science must play a part in order to keep the imagination under control. The imagination must play its part - possibly a greater one, since science cannot be part of the very real incidence of ghostly visitations and so on. At least not yet. 'Even science cannot attribute everything to malfunctioning livers and other disorders, and science,' thought Isabella as she walked slowly up the steps, 'would be pushed to explain why someone she disliked (and even feared a little) could nevertheless cause this feeling ... of being drawn ... however unwillingly, towards him.' Like him or not, there was this small pull; he was there, her tenant and she could not therefore entirely avoid seeing him even if only on market days - and she was involved. Some might even say - the serious researchers - that he had already put a 'frith' (free) or spell upon her ... and there was something menacing in the idea.

But *she* didn't come into any of the accredited categories. Isabella was neither a medium, a 'Taibhsear', nor a fortune teller, and though she possessed the superstitious beliefs said to be common to those of Celtic origin, she was not on the whole particularly imaginative. Living alone in a draughty and ancient castle whose electricity supply was erratic at the best of times she had felt, seen and heard nothing - until the night of the strange gathering. True, once in her room she preferred to stay there until morning, but that was because of the cold rather than fear of the supernatural. Angus was right. There were no ghosts at the castle. But she had been vouchsafed a glimpse into the past though she'd seen nothing, and that was relevant, as was the extraordinary - but so far purely beneficial - influence upon her of the Stone. Sitting on the wall in the sun, she thought deeply, and as she thought, a third thread began to interweave itself into the other two; herself; the Stone; and now Kenneth

Mackenzie. And the name of the seer so cruelly put to death by her ancestress had also been Kenneth Mackenzie.

That night brought with it an experience which she would never forget. Again she was woken at about the same time as on the former occasion, and with the moonlight on her face, by a sinister, mutedly angry murmur of voices, punctuated by bestial shouts - as though a crowd had gathered to witness a hanging - noises that were but an obbligato to tortured screams rising high above them. The sound didn't come from the house, nor from the park. That much Isabella realised before diving under the bedclothes, her hands pressed to her ears. But nothing could block out those dreadful, anguished, piercing screams - of a human soul in absolute agony ... nor the voice of Kenneth Mackenzie. She lay trembling, clutching the Stone until at last the sound began to fade. It returned, faded, returned much fainter, and at last vanished altogether. But it was almost morning before she finally slept again.

Now Isabella really was faced with a dilemma. Like her ancestress she was terribly troubled, equally convinced that the screams would go with her to her grave. As time passed she became less oppressed, trying with some success to put the matter out of her mind or to ascribe it to a dream. But there was too much of a coincidence. Like it or not the threads had become entwined through no fault of hers, and in order to regain her peace of mind she knew she would have to somehow disentangle them. She and the Stone could live together - possibly - though not, as seemed likely, if it were the agency by which she was being forced to admit Kenneth Mackenzie into her life, at the moment most violently, against her will. But if the Stone wouldn't release its hold on her, she must get rid of it. Another night like that one and she would go barmy. It was beyond a joke. But even as this thought occurred, she knew there would never be another. Those two occasions, not *déjà vu* so much as *déjà entendu* had been a sort of introduction; a prelude to events to follow. One thing was certain, or almost so, and that was that Kenneth might be descended from the original Seer. Two weeks later she had made up her mind. She had to know so she would go and ask him.

She chose the early afternoon and, realising that if she told him everything, or almost everything, he would want to see the Stone for himself, she removed it from her knickers and hung it round her neck on a ribbon in a little bag which had once held lavender, tucking it between her meagre breasts. Thoughtless she might be, but one thing one did not do was to fish about in one's knickers with a man looking on. Certainly not one with his reputation. With this in mind, she took her bicycle, though she had to push it almost all the way up the Rock and beyond to the Loch. Beyond that was a made-up road and if things turned out badly for her she would at least have the chance of getting away.

But there was something she had failed to take into account. When she arrived and rather timidly knocked on the front door of the little white-washed croft, he opened it and he was drunk. His face was red and he smelt of whisky, blowing out a great gust of spiritous breath as they confronted each other.

"If it isn't Miss Mackenzie," he exclaimed, opening the door wide with an exaggerated gesture and standing back for her to pass. "Well, I *am* honoured. Do come in." Isabella hesitated. Already she was feeling uncomfortable, wishing she hadn't come. She would rather have talked to him on the doorstep only a few paces from where her bicycle leant against the fence, but she hesitated only a second. She went in thinking she was a fool. She ought to have thought of this; rung him up; asked him to the castle; or something. She wasn't particularly alarmed; his behaviour had been perfectly alright on the other occasion when she had been alone with him, but it was going to make it difficult for her if he was too drunk to understand. After all it was no ordinary matter she had to discuss. She followed him into one of the only three rooms the little house seemed to possess. A kitchen on one side; another room over to her right; the open door disclosing an unmade bed.

"You must wonder at my coming to visit you like this," she said, sitting down on a kitchen chair as close to the door as possible. "I'm sorry I didn't telephone, or write and make an appointment, but there's something I must ask you about."

"Go ahead," he said. He had walked over to the fireplace and now stood with his arm along the mantelpiece. "What is it you need to know?"

"Well, I hope you won't think it very rude of me, but something has happened ... I mean ... well, it's like this. You've heard of the famous Seer - the one who made all those prophecies, a lot of which have come true. Are you ... ?" (It was difficult, this. Alexander Mackenzie, whose book has been in print ever since he wrote it in 1877, makes no mention of the Seer having married, or even that he existed at all. But if this was the case, how could the prophecies have been recorded?)

"Am I what? Descended from him? That's what you want to know, of course?"

Isabella nodded, blushing.

"And if I'm illegitimate? At least one of his descendants must have been. He didn't marry, we're told."

"I'm sorry."

"Oh, don't be. *I'm* not illegitimate," he lied, "though my father might have been." As he spoke he watched her warily, thinking that it might be worth his while to go along with this rubbish she seemed to find so important. Of course he had

63

heard about the Seer and dismissed it as of no interest, but it was not the moment to say so. He said carefully: "You see, I know quite a lot about it. It's interesting, isn't it?" She nodded, her eyes bright; pleased that he seemed to agree with her.

"Do tell me more," he begged. He turned his head away to conceal a yawn, but willing to see this through if it didn't take too long, because he might learn something to his advantage, even if only the next step to take.

Isabella told him. About the page from the journal, the finding of the Stone and its influence on her. Then she went on to speak of the strange visitations in the middle of the night. Her head was bent and she was concentrating on the effort of putting the tale into some logical order, speaking slowly to help him take it in. It was the sort of tale that needed a bit of concentration so she did not notice the look which had come across his face as she spoke. A look, half scornful, half indulgent, such as one might bestow upon a child with an exciting plan or idea ... anyone else but Kenneth Mackenzie, that is ... for there was something else in that look as well; something purely evil.

"Wait a minute: this stone. Have you really got it?"

"Of course." She caught hold of the ribbon round her neck, slipped it over her head, undid the bow round the bag and tipped the Stone out onto her palm. "You see! It's just as she said it was. Like an elfin moon; and it has lain at the back of that drawer for nearly three centuries. After the Black Priest had thrown it away, Isabella, my several times great grandmother, went down to the Ness and retrieved it from the sea."

He made no move to take it from her. He glanced at it indifferently; she watched him, aware at that moment he hadn't believed a word.

"At the Burning, I suppose. The Burning ... by your several times great grandmother of my several times great grandfather." (Now why had he said that? He'd never before given the matter a thought.)

"Well, he was a wicked man. He brought ruin to the family in the years after."

"But was he so wicked? It seems to me that he was merely giving her a straight answer to a straight question ... one which he hadn't wanted to answer in the first place ... " He stopped, suddenly realising that he was talking once again of something he knew hardly a thing about. Just that it might have happened.

There was no point in arguing with him. She half-got up to go.

"Do you really believe in all that stuff about prophecies?" he asked.

"Yes. Don't you?"

"Oh, possibly. I don't know. I can't see the relevance of them in those dreams you had, though." Isabella sat down again.

"They weren't dreams," she assured him earnestly. "I'm sure of it. They were too real ... those screams were too real."

"And it was my voice? Each time? You're sure of it?" Now he sounded more interested.

"Quite sure. I knew it the minute you started singing that ballad on the way home the other day. Before that I hadn't connected you with the voice. I suppose that was because I'd only met you once and we hadn't really had much time to talk."

"Strange. Perhaps you were thinking of me on each occasion. Thought transference or some such thing."

"I certainly wasn't. Why should I think of you?"

"You never know your luck. As for the screams, I suppose even I might be inclined to let out a yell or two if I were being burnt to death in a spiked tar barrel."

She could see he wasn't taking her seriously. Innocent as she was, she had no idea that he thought the whole thing a put-up job, an excuse to come and see him because she fancied him.

"But ... "

"Yes?"

She drew a deep breath and spoke with extreme reluctance.

"Well ... they say you ... that you do things with black magic ... or something. Someone saw blue lights from your back garden and ... and they heard screams ... as if an animal was in pain."

"Oh, I know I've got a reputation for being the Devil's Emissary. What else did they tell you? That I'd been fined for neglecting some sheep?"

"Yes."

"Couldn't help it. There was a hole in the fence and two of them got out and entangled themselves in bramble bushes. Just that. It happened during the night and the next day it started snowing very early in the morning, and by the time I'd noticed they were missing, the snow had piled up in such deep drifts I couldn't have got into the wood to look for them. No one's fault. And if a farmer's wife doesn't yet know the cries of a rabbit in a snare, it's time she did."

"So that's all it was?"

"Yes. But what is all this leading to? I mean how do you think I can relate my supposed descent from someone who hasn't yet been proved to have even existed, with your ... er ... nocturnal fancies?"

"But they *weren't* fancies. It all happened just as I've said."

"And I tell you they were. You Highlanders are all the same ... a bogle behind every whin, as the saying goes. Like a drink?" She shook her head, then changed her mind.

"Please, a little." He fetched a glass and poured some in from the bottle of whisky on the mantelpiece, handed it to her and then took a pull. Isabella took the glass, watching him.

"Oh, and of course. The fire and brimstone. Simple. I was burning some rubbish in the yard and something, salt probably, gave out a blue flame. I'd hardly qualify for the Worshipful Company of Warlocks on that alone. Satisfied?"

Yes, she thought. The dream part of it. That must have been the influence of Isabella's journal, combined with her finding of the Stone and the castle ... every ingredient was present for the making of a fine witches brew (or bree as Alison called it), of fanciful imaginings. She wasn't sure she liked the idea of Kenneth appearing in her dreams, in any form, but she was prepared to accept his account of the sheep and the trapped rabbit. Made bolder by the whisky she stared at him; thinking that he wasn't bad-looking. Tall, strong and with good features; if one could forget the sinister eyes ... He might be 'ower fond of the bottle' but he wasn't too drunk and he had behaved alright - so far. But then why shouldn't he? He obviously didn't like her anymore than anyone else did, she decided, the whisky making her momentarily self-pitying. And for the first time she found herself wishing rather that he did. From that moment she was no longer in control of her destiny. She had in fact been lost from the moment she had decided to trust him ... to accept his story of straying rabbits, snow and snared sheep ... or something like that, thought Isabella, as the whisky fumes soared to her brain. She looked up again. The eyes she thought she didn't like were watching her speculatively. Suddenly she was nervous. She looked quickly at her watch and jumped up.

"Heavens, how late it is!" she exclaimed theatrically. "I *must* go."

He made no move to stop her and as soon as she had mounted her bicycle and wobbled off down the track, he went back into the house and opened another bottle. She'd come back. No doubt about it. He wasn't bothered.

Isabella, her head whirling, rode home downhill on a cloud. Halfway between the croft and the castle she suddenly remembered the dog and every trace of intoxication promptly vanished.

Kenneth Mackenzie, though the name was self-bestowed, was of Scottish origin, the result of a chance encounter in a Glasgow alley between a drunk navvy and a Woolworth salesgirl. He had never known his real name and did not care for the one given to him at the orphanage where he was brought up.

He was by any reckoning a thoroughly bad lot. Nowadays he would have been diagnosed and treated as a dangerous psychopath, but at that state of the war there were few arrangements for people like him, and in the Navy into which he was conscripted and in which he spent the shortest possible time, he had appeared to be normal. But at the full moon he was liable to strange fits - the story of Dr. Jekyll and Mr. Hyde is after all based on fact - and he would go off and kill something. Sometimes he strangled a stray dog or cat; sometimes he would slit the throat of a horse or pony in a field. Had the Navy doctors not been so pressed at the time, or had he shown signs of abnormality in his medical examinations (or had they taken place at the full moon) things might have been different. But by 1940 when they needed every man they could get, especially the young, the tall and the strong, he could evade conscription no longer.

Six months later he jumped ship when she put in to Rosyth for a refit. He lay very low in Edinburgh for a while where he skulked in the red-light district living off a middle-aged prostitute, venturing out only after dark. He'd saved up his pay and in time, after he judged they'd given him up and marked him on the books as 'Run', he made the prostitute buy him an almost new suit and a couple of shirts, shoes and underwear and a set of papers informing the interested that he was now Kenneth Mackenzie with a reserved occupation as a slaughterhouse worker. Overnight William Johnson ceased to be and Kenneth Mackenzie had hitched a lift to Stranraer, from whence he caught a ferry to Larne and within a week had found a job in a slaughterhouse in the heart of Ireland, as far away from any naval base as he could get and where his skill was more than once remarked upon.

The mental condition of such as he brings with it a natural cunning and very often a good deal of intelligence, for such people are seldom the low-browed imbeciles of popular thinking. On the contrary their intelligence is often above average (which is why the condition is so difficult to detect); likewise their sense of perception - all heightened by the abnormality and especially, for some as yet unexplained reason, at the full moon.

The work in the slaughterhouse suited him and as no questions were asked, nobody needed to know that he had never done this work before in his life. He lived in digs in the small market town, walked to work, no great distance, and when not required, devoted his time to learning how to improve his speech, which eventually became almost accentless. He'd done well at school, learned easily and was able to read fluently and write basic sentences at six. Why he wanted to improve himself in this manner was something he didn't understand himself. His instincts told him to and he always obeyed his instincts. They'd never let him down yet and something told him that one day other things might. So he bought himself a small wireless and copied to himself the accents of the announcers and readers.

But ... he started to drink and in drinking became careless.

Then, after a slack period in the slaughterhouse, he was

nearly caught one night at the full moon in the act of slitting the throat of a tethered pony belonging to the gypsies on the common. The war now in its final stages, he signed on as deckhand on a trawler and finally returned to Scotland via Lewis. He would have stayed there had there been work for him, for he felt a strange affinity to the place - as though he'd lived there long before. But there was no work. Back on the mainland his skill with animals made him much in demand as a stockworker, for there was still a shortage all over Scotland, for the local men had not yet returned or never would, while the Italian and German prisoners who had supplied so much of the labour force during the war were being returned to their native lands. Thus Kenneth had no difficulty in getting jobs on big estates where his fair looks and pleasant, educated manner made him acceptable. Then a spate of mysterious throat cuttings and stranglings (which were never connected with him; he was much too circumspect now) decided him to move on - each time with a reference in his pocket testifying to the excellence of his work with stock ... which it was when the moon was merely gibbous or on the wane. And so he came to the castle, and having saved up a good deal of his pay and the previous lone tenant of the croft having recently died, he'd persuaded Angus to rent the tenure to him. Angus had been delighted that the new tenant was yet another Mackenzie ... to begin with. When he got to know Kenneth better he was less sure ... there was something about him that made him uneasy. By the time Kenneth came to meet Isabella he had been her tenant for nearly a year.

The next time he went to market he went into the lending library and took out a copy of the prophecies of the Seer that the girl had talked such gibberish about. For he thought he knew now how best to fix his interest with her and this was beginning to be something he wanted to do very much. For all that she was as ugly as a witch and had about as much sex appeal as one of his own sheep, it had not escaped his calculating mind that Isabella as his wife, rather than his landlord, would be a much better deal. Deep down, while outwardly courteous, he hated the privileged landowners with their money and belongings and great castles, even though most of the ones he had known were falling, like this place, rapidly to bits. Now the opportunity had come his way for him to be a laird himself. No longer a poor tenant trying to make a small living on impossible ground - quite different from the rich barley and oat fields held by the luckier tenants below the castle and over the river. But he'd have to hurry. She could be snapped up at any moment by a member of the hated gentry. The fact that the inheritance must remain Isabella's and her children's and probably could not be disposed of unless she died childless, when the Trust would automatically be wound up, did not bother him. He thought it would be something of the sort and resolved, when he saw her again, to try and find out just how matters stood. He could trust her, he thought, his mouth curling into a sneer, to blurt out the answers to things he wanted to know. He knew how he could make her talk. Not that there should be any need. She'd already visited him off her own bat, much against, if he wasn't mistaken, Angus and Alison Stewart's advice, and had shown no reticence in telling him of her old Seer. Yes, that was the way to set about it. He must read the book so as to have all the answers ready. He must pretend to know it all, much more than she. Like that the silly little fool would be impressed.

Back at home, he opened a bottle of whisky and sat down with it handy on a small, stained table beside him, the better to find out all he could about this ridiculous person ... prophesying and whatnot all of three hundred years ago. He soon grew

71

bored, decided he'd just do the local prophecies - the ones concerning the family and the castle and trust to luck she wouldn't want to talk about the others. But when he came to the bit about the Seer's stone he grew thoughtful, even interested. Hadn't she already shown him a stone which had magical properties or some such thing and which she had found at the back of a desk? Yes, that could be a way to bring her back. She'd have to come to him though. There were far too many busybodies in the vicinity of the castle who'd be sure to make it their business to put the word about that Kenneth Mackenzie was visiting Miss Isabella.

He would write to her and say how interested he'd been in her story ... no, he couldn't say that. He'd obviously shown her he didn't believe a word, and though he'd been quick-witted enough in claiming descendancy from the Seer, she just might not be as gullible as he would like - or he'd first thought her. And it wouldn't do to bungle it. She hadn't seemed to fall immediately under his spell. He must be careful. He took a long pull at the whisky bottle. Yes. Very, very careful.

So he wrote his letter, the next day when he was quite sober, saying that he had forgotten while she was there - so much else to talk about - to ask her to let him see the Stone properly. He knew the story so well, but had thought, like everyone else, that the real stone had been thrown into what was now Loch Ussie on the occasion of the Seer's last and most fateful (to her family) prophecy. It would be so kind of her if she could make the journey to his house, so as to avoid gossip, in order that he could see and handle the magic stone for himself. Would next Thursday be convenient? At about the same time as last? He thought, reading the letter through, it sounded interesting enough to bring her to him.

It was the sort of letter, pompous and rather obsequious, that a man of his type, wishing to impress, would write, but

72

Isabella saw nothing odd in it. She was pleased at his interest, hoping that after all he might be able to throw some light on her extraordinary visitations. She still didn't know if she liked him but she wanted to show someone her stone. And if he really was a descendant however wrong-sided the blanket had been, it might even possess magical properties for him. It was rather like going to a fortune teller, only better, she decided, as she pushed her bicycle up the Rock.

He was waiting for her, watching as she came into view, breasting the long, steep ascent to his gate. He felt restless and irritated; he'd been out all morning rounding up straying sheep - one, an old ewe, had fallen down a gully and was stuck upended. He had left it there and now he was in no mood to go along with this unattractive beanpole of a girl and her whimsies. The moon was nearly full. Soon now he would go out and kill, a long way from here - on the road to Inverness and then spend the rest of the night in a drunken stupor, probably in the arms of some whore or other. The mood was strongly upon him and he greeted her shortly as she came to the door. But he must be careful. A lot depended on this meeting. It was a pity that it should have to be now, at this time.

Isabella answered him in a slightly constrained manner. He did not look pleased to see her and somewhere in her head there sounded a little warning voice. Be careful; be careful, it seemed to say. Once more she recalled the dog. Of course she could have been mistaken, half-hoping she was.

He stood back to show her in. She went before him and sat down on the sofa with its shabby, cat-shredded upholstery. It smelt of tom cat too, but though she looked about her, there were no cats in the room, nor any sign of a resident one.

"Well," he said, somewhat impatiently. "Aren't you going to show me your famous stone? Have you really got it or are you making all this up?" He tried to speak jokingly, but there was a grating sound in his voice. She heard it and looked up at him indignantly.

"But of course I've got it. You've already seen it, only you weren't interested."

She caught hold of the ribbon round her neck, undid the bow and tipped the stone out onto her palm.

"As I told you last time, it's just as they said it was. Like an elfin moon, and it's lain at the back of that drawer for nearly three centuries. You see, after the Black Priest had thrown it away, Isabella, my several times great grandmother went down to the Ness and retrieved it. Remember?"

"At the Burning? ... The Burning, by your several times great grandmother of my several times great grandfather." (Hadn't he said that before?)

"Well, he was a wicked man. He brought ruin on the family in the years after. I told you all this last time."

"And I told you he was merely giving her a straight answer to a straight question. He had to say something. I don't call that wicked. It wasn't him who caused all those things to happen. He only said they would. And he hadn't wanted to answer the question in the first place, but like all women she nagged and pestered so much that he had to say something to keep her quiet. She was the wicked one. Not him. The aristocracy are always right; surely you've found that out by now? It's always us poor devils who are in the wrong." He sounded very bitter and Isabella began to feel uncomfortable and to wish strongly she hadn't come.

He bent his head, peering at the Stone.

"That's not it. The real one was supposed to be black with a hole in it. It was 'cam' or one-eyed."

"I know. But it must have been this one or she wouldn't have rescued it and kept it and thought of it as having magic properties."

He asked "Can I look at it?" He held out his hand but she immediately closed her fingers tightly over it. She hesitated. "I can't let you have it ... to hold, I mean. I can't explain why but I must keep it on me all the time."

"I shouldn't have thought a minute or two would have made all that difference. Come on. I can't see it properly in your hand. It's too dark in here. Anyway," he added, trying to suppress his irritation (for some reason it seemed extraordinarily important that he should have the stone in his possession) "how can I believe in your tales of magic if you won't let me try and find out for myself?"

"Oh very well then. But you must give it back to me the moment I ... the moment I ask for it."

He was not listening. His fingers were clenching and working at the stone, kneading it like a piece of dough. His eyes were blank and glassy and his breath came in short gasps and at that moment, Isabella gazing at him, terrified, was conscious of the presence of an evil force so strong it was almost tangible, realising that he was in the throes of some sort of fit or seizure. How could she know that Kenneth Mackenzie, soi-disant descendant of the legendary Seer had just been given a licence to kill? Nor would it be animals any longer. That instinct present in most men, kept hidden and tamed, had now overpowered him, and from that moment he was a very dangerous person indeed.

The fit passed. He relaxed, felt fumblingly for the whisky bottle, tilted it to his lips and drank it like water, in great gulping swallows. Isabella would have liked some too to steady her nerves. Most of all though she wanted the Stone to be given back to her so she could be on her way. Now she wanted nothing more to do with him. That awful look had frightened her more than anything in her life.

"I'd like it back now," she said, trying to keep her voice from trembling. "Unless you want to go on prophesying. Were you prophesying?" she asked curiously, unable to resist the question. What had made him look like that at that moment ... as though he'd had a vision of something from the Pit?

He sat down on the sofa and stared at her. His eyes still looked very peculiar, flat and expressionless, like boiled sweets. She watched him slip the stone into his pocket and shake his head. Furiously angry she lunged at him.

"Give me my Stone. Give it back to me, damn you," she shouted. "It's mine. I tell you, you're to give it back." He fended her off easily.

"Oh no. And it's not yours. It was taken from him by force ... stolen in fact by one of those bloody aristocratic forbears of yours. It's mine now and I'm going to keep it. Do you hear? ... I'm going to keep it." His voice was slurred, but he was still in command and, as she leapt at him again, almost crying, he seized her wrists and pushing her violently onto the floor, threw himself on top of her. His kilt was no barrier, but her regulation issue knickers were. Tearing at them, he felt the elastic give. He dragged them down with one hand, holding her down by the hair with the other, his chest pinning her to the floor. She kicked and struggled against the animal force which held her, but fit and strong though she was, he was by far the stronger. Now he was shoving something between her clamped legs. He tore them apart; she shut her eyes; felt the ... it ... high up. A moment's searing pain and it was deep inside her and as he moved, grunting obscenely, he slightly relaxed the iron hold on her hair. She tore it from him, raised her head and tried to bite him, but her teeth met only the rough wool of his shirt.

Now he was shoving away, hurting her cruelly and already it was too late. His body shuddered in a gasping climax and he relaxed still further, momentarily off guard. Isabella, wriggling from under him, managed to get her left arm from where it had been stuck uselessly under the sofa, was on her fleet in a flash. She kicked off her knickers, grabbed her remaining shoe and was gone, her Stone forgotten. (But at least she'd escaped with her life, luckier than the prostitute who turned up two days later on a piece of wasteland in Glasgow, strangled and with her throat cut.)

Kenneth Mackenzie propped himself up on his elbow and got slowly to his feet. He made no move to go after her, but she'd come back. His eyes fell on her knickers still on the floor. He smiled unpleasantly. Oh yes, she'd come back alright. He'd made sure of *that* - on two counts.

Now the cold fingers of the wind reached up, drying impartially both tears and the only half-comprehended but wholly alien stickiness, the legacy of that brutal initiation.

Horror, shock, disgust - the usual aftermath of a rape - were soon swamped by Isabella's distress at the loss of her Stone, though it so easily could have been her life. Without it she felt as though a part of her had gone, together with her integrity and maidenhood ... a tiny but vital bit of her, so that its loss was almost a physical sensation of bereavement and of deprivation. For two days she stayed at home in a state of shock, spending much of her time lying on her bed thinking; deeply ashamed, so that like a hurt animal which crawls away to die, all she wanted was to be left alone. Anyway without the Stone she seemed to have no volition; no motivating force; no desire to do anything. She rang up Alison the next day and told her she had caught a cold and didn't want to pass it on to either of them - a lame enough excuse, but it served. Alison, worried, offered her food, but was staved off.

She slept for many hours, through most of the following

day and night and in the morning youth and strength reasserting their combined influence, she felt better; got up and went to lunch with the Stewarts as usual. If they noticed anything in her manner to cause them concern, they gave no sign of it and Isabella was able to congratulate herself on a good performance. True, she was a little abstracted from time to time, having to have remarks repeated to her, and when they discussed the murder in Glasgow, the announcement of which had appeared in the local press that day, she did not seem to take it in.

As the days succeeded each other she ceased to feel the loss of the Stone quite so acutely, as another worry intruded itself. The moon waned and twenty-one days later Isabella, increasingly distraught, looked for the signs that, once dreaded, she now longed for with all her soul. But the elfin moon was born, waxed and there was no sign of her curse. And then she knew that unless something happened to prevent it, in about eight months time a child would be born to her. A child with a monster for a father.

A week later she had to get up in a hurry in the early morning to be sick and even she, previously totally unacquainted with such matters, too lacking in interest to be bothered to find out, was going to have to face a few unpleasant facts. For she meant to get rid of the baby. One could as long as it wasn't left too late. Scraps of giggling conversations between her cousins, overheard and unconsciously assimilated, began to come back to her. Gin, hot baths, jumping off heights and, as a last resort, knitting needles, were among the curious measures apparently resorted to by unfortunate young women who found themselves 'in trouble'. Well, she was one of the unfortunates now. In very great trouble. Soon everyone would know and the disgrace would be intolerable. Alison and Angus, her two friends who had devoted their lives to her interests, would be mortified and ashamed on her behalf. It would never be forgotten. Not in the feudal, God-fearing Scotland of the time when John Knox's spirit still brooded censoriously and the woman was always in the wrong. This *must* not happen. Even if she had to kill herself, she was not going to have this baby. A baby with a monster for a father. It too would be a monster. She knew that as certainly as night would continue to succeed day.

She considered the proven remedies. Hot baths, except in Alison's house, were out of the question because the wood was so wet the geyser wouldn't produce more than a trickle of lukewarm water. She didn't dare ask in the Control (the off-licence) for gin. They might wonder ... and she baulked at the knitting needle, not knowing exactly what to do. There remained jumping off high walls. But even this had to be done carefully in case someone should see her and wonder. She found a lot of wine in the cellar, but it made her sick - as if she wasn't already ... every morning. After a few days of this she made up her mind to go to London. There she was sure she could get the job done and no one would be the wiser.

A fortnight later another strangled prostitute turned up in a dark alleyway in Dundee, her throat cut from ear to ear ... and Isabella began to wonder. Somehow, she thought, these murders are connected - with each other - and with Kenneth Mackenzie, and as the realisation came to her, there came also the possibility that she might be the next victim. Still she wasn't afraid; not now that she had faced the possibility. For a moment she considered the idea of asking if she could stay with the Stewarts at the next full moon, but rejected the idea as too difficult. All sorts of questions would be asked and the answers could only sound ridiculous. In any case this man was her fate. She couldn't run away from that. It was a possibility she was able to put from her - unlike her other, far greater problem - because it was real. She'd made up her mind she was not going to bring his child into the world and she was going to be revenged on him as soon as she could. A visit to London became, not just an idea, but an absolute necessity. As to the other thing: she could take precautions and she would probably be safe enough until the next full moon, by which time she would have gone.

Another pressing need was the return of the Stone, and for this she would have to tell the Stewarts, for she would have to have Angus' help. In any case she couldn't go away for an indefinite period without giving them some reason which would be acceptable to them; nor could she slip away carrying a suitcase and explain later. Someone might see her and wonder ... and tell them. She owed them an explanation. Another thing; she'd left her bicycle at the croft (she had been much to sore to ride it) and didn't feel like a three mile walk to the nearest bus stop.

Her mind made up, she packed her suitcase next morning, put it outside on the verandah and walked gingerly, for she was still very sore, up to the Lodge.

At lunch she said carefully to Angus: "I wonder ... er ... could you take me to the station this afternoon. I've decided to go to London for a bit. It's a long time since I've seen my aunt and cousins ... and I'd like to do a bit of shopping. Perhaps I shall buy myself a small car, then I shouldn't have to depend on you so much Angus."

There was a short silence.

"Why, Miss Bella," replied Angus heartily, "it's a pleasure tae tak ye aboot. But ye're no looking as bonny as ye were a while syne. Ye could dae wi' a wee holiday I'm thinking. I'll fetch yer wee bag later on and after we've had our tea I'll rin ye tae the station ... unless ye'd like me tae tak ye tae Inverness?"

"Oh no. I can easily get the connection. We mustn't waste petrol."

"Have ye made a reserrvation? It's a sleeper ye'll be needing I'm thinking."

"Yes. No. I only made up my mind this morning. It's awfully kind of you. I know it's short notice ... but I can't tell you now ... I will some day ... but not yet. But I must go immediately. It's so important. Do please forgive me." She was nearly in tears, only just holding on to control and sanity.

Husband and wife glanced at each other. 'She looks haunted, the puir lassie,' Angus thought. 'She's lost her bonny looks.' In fact Isabella had lost weight again, a thing which happened very easily to her, and she had the gaunt and haggard appearance of someone with a great deal (mostly unpleasant) on her mind, with greenish-black circles round her eyes and mouth. Distressed, he got up and patted her hand. He glanced again at Alison, who made a small, dismissive movement. He nodded and went out of the room.

"Now what's the trouble, dearie. Can you not tell Alison? Angus is in the right of it. You'll always look bonny to me but it's true you're not looking well."

"I'm alright, Alison; I am really," she said wildly. There was a short pause.

"Oh, Alison, I've done something so dreadful ... " She tried to smile ... "well, perhaps not dreadful - just stupid. But promise me not to tell anyone else. Nobody but you and Angus must ever know. For one thing it ... well, it sounds so silly and for another ... you warned me not to have anything to do with him and I didn't listen to you. At least I did, but he seemed alright, and then I had these queer visions ... no, not visions, because I didn't actually see him ... but I heard him ... I *heard* him, Alison ... twice. Kenneth Mackenzie, I mean. So I thought I'd go and see if he was in any way connected with the Kenneth Mackenzie of Isabella's day ... the Seer. I know it sounds peculiar ... or just improbable, but it was so *real*."

And she told Alison most of the story, only omitting the assault upon herself. She couldn't bring herself to confess even to this dear, kind person who was her best friend - she was too ashamed. She couldn't burden either of them with this knowledge and after all, it could have been at least partly her fault. She'd thrown herself at him - in a rage - but perhaps he hadn't perfectly understood. He'd tried to fend her off ... and why on earth was she now making excuses for him when there were none? He'd taken her Stone and refused to give it back.

"I *must* have it back, Alison. I can't live properly without it." She paused. Then heard herself saying strange things: "without it I am lost in a world that has no edges, no permanency, where I may slip and slide between the ages and never find firm footing ... " as though she was reciting.

"What's that you're saying my bairn?" enquired Alison, puzzled.

Isabella started. "I don't know," she replied slowly ... I don't know why I said that ... or said it like that. But I must have it. If I went back I know he wouldn't give it to me ... he'd just think I fancied him or something ... "

"And you don't dearie," asked Alison very quietly.

"No, *no, NO!*" burst out Isabella. "I hate him; I wouldn't have gone back, only he wrote asking if he could see the Stone. He's evil ... " Then she told Alison about the dog. "I know he meant to run it over. He had a sort of look on his face. Alison, do you think he's mad?"

"He could be. After all, none of us knows much about him."

"But I must have my Stone. I need it so much ... it makes everything alright for me ... lovely and happy ... which it never was before and isn't again now I've lost it." She looked ravaged. Alison patted her hand.

"Angus'll get it for you, dearie. And you say you left

82

your bicycle there. Why was that?"

Isabella blushed. "I left it in a hurry," she almost whispered, hanging her head. "He looked so ... well, so angry ... and he was drunk ... and I forgot it. I thought he'd come after me."

Angus took her to the station, saw her onto the train and promised he'd do all he could to recover the stone. Unlike Alison he had a very shrewd idea of what might have taken place. Kenneth Mackenzie, drunk, had made a pass at the girl as if she were any common trollop and she'd naturally rejected him. 'But we warned the lassie,' he thought, shaking his head sadly. 'We both warned her.'

The next day Angus drove up the Rock to the croft and seeing the door open walked in. The first thing he saw were Isabella's navy blue knickers draped over the back of the sofa.

He stood there, thinking swiftly, then called through the open kitchen door: "Are ye there, Mackenzie. It's Stewart."

Kenneth came in from the bothy at the back of the house wearing a scowl. "Oh, it you," he said unpleasantly. "Before you tell me why you're here, perhaps you will tell me if you always walk into people's houses when the front door is open?"

"Only if they've something to hide," replied Angus amiably. "I've come to collect Miss Isabella's belongings. I hear she left a wheen things here the other afternoon, including her bicycle. I wonder noo why she didna' ride it hame. Sae I'll tak that and the ither things," and he made a movement of his hand towards Isabella's knickers. Kenneth looked black.

Angus walked to the sofa, picked up the knickers and put them in his pocket.

"Anything else?" he asked. Kenneth jerked his head in the direction of Isabella's bicycle leaning against the wall of the croft.

"And her wee stane?" asked Angus. "She'll no be best pleased with me if I return wi'out her stane."

Kenneth fished it out of his pocket. Angus took it from him without making contact. Then he asked:

"And what did ye do to Miss Bella to make her leave in a hurry without a sairtain article of apparel, her bicycle and her wee stane, is what I'm wondering?"

"Nothing she didn't ask for," replied Kenneth with a sneer which made Angus long to hit him. "And I'm sure you're wondering too if she was a virgin, aren't you? Like all the other men here. Well, she is ... was."

Had Angus been a younger man he'd have felled this bastard with one blow. Instead he said:

"And what if ye've made her pregnant? Had ye thocht o' that?"

"Of course; I probably have. She'll have to marry me, won't she?"

"Will she? I'm wondering if she's wishful to. I didna' get the impression that she likit ye ower much. Still and on if she's wishful tae wed ye, it's no consairn of mine; but one thing, I'm telling ye, Kenneth Mackenzie, if ye let ane word of this pass your dirty mouth to a single soul I'll hae ye oot o' here. I'll tell Mr. Wotherspoon what's to pass. Aye and I'll see tae it that naebody in the North will tak ye on as tenant ever again. So ye'd better gang to England." He took a step towards the door and paused, looking back over his shoulder and said: "Forbye, I'm wondering what garred ye tae think yer advances wad be welcome? I dinna see Miss Bella as the kind o' lassie that'll throw hersel' at anyin."

"Oh. Didn't you know that Mackenzie women are said to be the best whores in the Highlands? Besides, that's exactly what she did do."

"I doot it was because she was ettling to be in yer airms,

84

Kenneth Mackenzie, for a' that. Come noo, man. Tell me the truth. I'll have it a' sooner or later."

"She was trying to get at her stone."

"And instead of gieing it her, ye rapit her? Is that so?"

"I tell you that was what she was after. Like all women. She was just using the stone as an excuse."

"I doot it. And d'ye ken why she's so unco' fond of yon stone?"

"She thinks it's the Seer's stone and gives those who own it the power to ... "

"Tae prophesy and sich?"

"Yes. Such rubbish."

"Ay, indeed. Aweel, guid day to ye, Mackenzie, and dinna forget - ane word of this and ye'll be oot on yer lug."

"Oh, really?" replied the young man, again with that contemptuous sneer. "And once I'm married to Miss Mackenzie, it'll be you, Mr. Angus Stewart, who'll be 'oot on yer lug'."

"Ay," replied Angus equably; "a' we have to dae is to wait on the day." He raised his hat and walked away down the path.

Kenneth stood looking after him, still with the contemptuous look darkening his face. That awful accent; why couldn't the man talk English? But despite the fact that he was a tenant and the factor only an employee, he was still in awe of the older man. After a while his brow lightened. He went back into the croft and sat down on the sofa with the whisky bottle beside him. On the whole things were going quite well. He'd been pretty thorough, he thought coarsely, remembering. A normal young woman should have no difficulty in conceiving. Oh, yes, *that* part of it had gone off well. And when she was certain she was pregnant he would ask her to marry him. The tenants might be surprised and not best pleased, but she'd have no choice. Public opinion could not possibly be outraged. Anybody else ... but not Isabella Mackenzie. She would marry him and if she didn't like him, that was just too bad. She should have thought of that sooner. And once he was the laird, he thought, his mind going ahead ... once all those Trusts were wound up, there'd be money, plenty of money. Money for whisky and for women. Other women, for it was not to be expected that someone with a face like hers and a scarecrow for a figure would hold onto him for long.

As for the stone ... for a moment he wished he'd said he'd lost it, instead of handing it over so tamely. But on the whole he was glad he had it no more. There had been something ... an incident ... connected, however tenuously, with that stone. He wasn't sure what it was but the presence of it in his hand gave him a strange sensation which had lead to others. His hands round a bare neck, choking the life out of its owner and ... the knife point sinking into a throat ... drawn, left and back, then right, and torrents of blood gushing down the naked breasts. That had been his favourite job in the slaughterhouse. After the animal had been stunned, it would then have the pithing rod pushed into the hole made by the stunning gun, and he would take over, shackle the hind legs and turn the wheel which raised the carcass onto the hooks hanging from the ceiling. Then he would slit the throat, revelling in the blood cascading over his boots. Those had been good times. Now ... well, now he didn't want to jeopardise his chances and he was beginning to wonder if the whisky wasn't making him just a little careless.

Angus went home with rage and despair in his heart. He had no doubt that in his absence yesterday Isabella had told Alison something of her predicament. He wondered how much. For his part he had no difficulty in believing that Isabella had made no advances which could have possibly been misinterpreted by anybody who hadn't an excellent reason for doing so. But what now? If only she hadn't gone back a second time ...

He looked so grim when Alison came in from the garden and found him sitting at the kitchen table staring before him, his hands lightly clasped that she was alarmed. Immediately she knew it was something far more serious than Isabella's silly little stone. Then she saw the navy blue knickers sticking out of his pocket.

As she pulled them out with an exclamation, he looked up.

"Aye. Alison, my doo. If ainly the lassie had heedit our warning." He shook his head.

She made them tea, then sat down and put her trembling hand on his. Her face was white.

"She doesna' like him Angus. But she'll marry him if he asks her. To avoid the scandal and give her bairn a father, if there is one. If you ask me he's had this in his mind ever since he first met her. And she an innocent. And with no mother to tell her about such things. That aunt of hers ... the feckless body ... "

"Aweel, it's nae tae see her aunt that she's gone to London for this time, Alison. It's a doctor she's gone for."

KEITH

In London Isabella found herself a small family hotel off Sloane Square, as far as possible from Durrants, where Aunt Kitty and the cousins always stayed, and booked a room for a week. Then she didn't know what to do next. Or rather how was she going to find the sort of doctor she needed. And what about a pseudonym? Her own name, Miss Mackenzie, was necessary for the hotel register because of letters from Angus and Alison. The same afternoon of her arrival, she caught a bus to Notting Hill Gate and in a seedy junk shop bought a little silver ring for ten shillings, putting it on the third finger of her right hand.

She walked back to the hotel as fast as she could, deep in thought. It was maddening trying to walk in London, constantly swerving this way and that; being brought up short and never being able to use the long stride that took her so effortlessly round her acres at home ... which if things didn't work out for her, she might never see again. She must find a doctor immediately.

She went back to the hotel and after looking through several telephone directories found the address of a hospital in the King's Road. She drank a cup of tea, ate a biscuit and set out again. The bus deposited her almost outside the building. Pausing only to transfer the ring to her left hand, she marched through the doors and up to the Reception Desk.

"I would like to make an appointment to see a doctor ... a gynaecologist," she said, rather breathlessly, and waited.

"I see," said the woman behind the desk. "Have you not got a family doctor who would find one for you?"

"No. I don't live in London."

89

"But where do you live? Isn't there someone ... ?"

Isabella shook her head. The woman thought, 'another of them,' but without emotion. She was too used to being asked for appointments with gynaecologists ... also to the results of requests for abortions being refused. It was after all illegal. The back street abortionists did a roaring trade in those days. She glanced at Isabella. Not quite the usual type.

"Well, dear, there's Doctor Mackenzie. He comes here on Thursday. Or perhaps you'd like to make an appointment yourself to see him at his house. He practises in Wimpole Street. He's expensive," she added, "but we could put you on the panel. It would mean waiting though, and might not be as satisfactory."

Isabella did not need to enquire into the meaning of that. She thanked the woman and walked out of the hospital and all the way back. At least she wasn't short of money. Perhaps she could bribe this Doctor Mackenzie or something.

Two days later she was ringing the bell under the brass plaque which said Dr. Keith Mackenzie, one of several on the wall of the tall house in Wimpole Street.

She was terribly nervous and waiting on the step remembered to transfer her little ring to the left hand only just in time.

She sat in the waiting room looking at a table covered with copies of the Tatler, The Illustrated London News, Country Life and all the usual trappings of the smart London doctor who can afford to put in a day a week for the benefit of the panel patients in hospital. When she saw him, Dr. Keith Mackenzie was, she decided, not too bad, in spite of his name. He rose and smiled at her as she was shown in by the nurse ... and memory stirred a small coal. He had seen the girl before.

"What can I do for you, Mrs. Mackenzie?" he asked, thinking something along the same lines as the receptionist at the hospital, only prepared to give her the benefit of the doubt.

Isabella sat down slowly and looked down at her hands.

She began, rather pointedly he thought, to rotate the little ring on her third finger. No engagement ring, he noticed. Oh dear.

"I'm ... " she began, " ... I mean, I think I'm going to have a baby."

"When was your last period?" he asked and was hardly surprised when she gave him the exact date. Had she but known it, the ultimate give-away: young married bliss seldom, in his experience, taking account of dates when otherwise engaged. Perhaps she wasn't newly married. Or happily. That would account for her haggard look and nervous gestures and the way she kept twisting that rather ordinary-looking ring. And she was too thin.

"Well," he said paternally. "I expect you'd like to know for certain. It's a bit early but I may be able to help you. I'll make an examination if you'd like to go with Nurse." There was nothing Isabella would have liked less. The nurse was middle-aged, grim-faced, with bristly grey hair and a slight moustache. The perfect chaperon for a young and, Isabella suddenly realised, not only extremely good-looking but *nice* doctor. She undressed her lower half and lay down on the high, narrow couch. The nurse drew a pink blanket over her and left her.

She had no idea what to expect. Deeply embarrassed she drew her legs up and apart as instructed and shut her eyes tightly. Dear God, *that* again ... so soon. Painful, humiliating, degrading and dreadfully embarrassing, but at least only hands this time.

He was quick and gentle and his impartial and unemotional exploration of her cringing interior didn't hurt nearly as much as she had expected. Her eyes remaining so tightly shut that small wrinkles appeared all round them, she did not see the look he gave the nurse at one stage in the brief examination, and it was with tightly compressed lips that he returned to his consulting-room without glancing at her again. Dear God, he too was thinking. Whatever sort of a man is she married to ... if she *is* married. If not ... and he thought he knew exactly what her next words would be.

But she surprised him. When he said: "You're about nine weeks pregnant. It should be born in the late summer ... ," she interrupted:

"You know I'm not married," she said suddenly. "I can always tell when people know things. I'm not Mrs. Mackenzie, I'm Miss. Isabella Mackenzie."

"Well, we're Mackenzies both." He gave her a delightful smile. "Are you just another one like me? You don't look it," (hoping to get her to talk a bit; confide in him.) She shook her head.

"Not quite."

"Oh, which are you? Cromarty, Scatwell, Gairloch ... goodness they go on for ever. I can't think of any more ... oh yes ... Assynt?"

She told him, unaware of the pride and love which sang in her voice as she pronounced the name.

"But this is terrific," he said. "So *you* are the laird? Or, ...?"

"Yes, I am ... but ... ? Do you know it?"

"I've been there once. I've got some sort of connection with the family from quite a long way back, and about three years ago I was on leave ... on my way north for some fishing and I thought I'd look in. Something I've always wanted to do ... to see the castle."

"Oh. And what did you think of it? Very ugly, as I did when I first saw it? I don't now."

"Very special. And I was lucky because I went to the lodge - one of them - in this case the factor's house - to ask permission to drive down to the castle. I found the factor at home ... a most delightful man. He was so interested to hear of

92

the connection, though it is a bit remote, that he offered to show me round and ... " he broke off. "Great Scott! Now I know where I've seen you before."

"You have?" she asked, her brows wrinkling. "But I don't remember ... "

"You wouldn't, and I haven't really. I meant the portrait in the drawing-room of the third Countess. Isabella, like yourself. And so like you."

"Yes. She was my several times great-grandmother."

"That's it then. But I thought that the castle belonged to someone else; a much older woman who lives in France."

"It did. My mother. But she died two years ago and it's now mine. One of those Scottish female inheritances. And you? Where do you come in?"

"I'll tell you, but not now," he said a little repressively, aware somewhat belatedly of another patient waiting; of a wholly unprofessional reluctance to have to abandon this conversation; and of shoals ahead. "I've another patient due in a few minutes and we must see what we can do for you. I take it ... you won't mind if I speak frankly ... saves time ... that you don't want this baby very much?"

"No. I don't. And I don't intend to have it. I'll ... "

"And the father? Does he know about it?"

"No. But he could suspect."

"And you don't want to marry him?"

"No." Isabella said shortly, her eyes glittering. "Nothing will make me marry him. At least not willingly ... but in order to avoid scandal I would have to marry somebody. Only there isn't anybody except him. I *must* get rid of this baby. I *must*. I can't marry him. Please help me." There was something else in her voice other than just panic, he decided. She sounded as if she hated the man, perhaps not without reason.

"Forgive me ... " he said, "I must be frank and you must

93

be truthful. Forget we're relations." Again the charming smile. "Remember only that I'm your doctor. You don't sound as if you liked this man, yet you are to have his baby? A bit contradictory, isn't it?"

"He ... he ... assaulted me."

"Oh. There's just one question I must ask you, though it's hardly my business, but it is essential for me to know if I'm to help you terminate this pregnancy - if I'm right in thinking that's what you're about to ask me. Did you give him any encouragement? So often when this happens it is rare that there hasn't been some sort of inducement. In some states of mind, as you know, the smallest look or provocative gesture is enough. A sign of willingness, you might say. Did you ... ?"

"I flung myself at him," was the surprising answer. "Twice. He wouldn't give me back my Stone. I suppose I lost my temper or something ... "

"Your ... stone?" And she told him the whole story, leaving nothing out while his next patient, well into the sixth month of her fourth pregnancy and glad to be off her feet, caught up with the social news in the waiting-room.

At the end of the story he stood up and held out his hand.

"I'll be in touch," was all he said. "It may take a few days ... it could be difficult to arrange ... it usually is and we've got to have a good case ... but come and see me again. Make an appointment as you go out," he added, clearly for the benefit of the nurse who opened the door at that moment to give him a dour look and remind him of the time.

He took a deep breath, resumed his professional manner and put Isabella's difficulty from him. But what an extraordinary tale. Nor had he the least doubt that she was telling the truth in its essentials. The Stone part of this far-fetched tale was nonsense, of course; pure fantasy.

94

Back at the hotel Isabella was opening a little parcel containing the Stone and the same night the visions started again. A man standing on a piece of waste with his hands round a woman's neck. As he laid her down on the ground, he took something out of his pocket and with a sweeping, semi-circular movement drew it under her chin from one ear to the other. Then the vision faded and was replaced with another. The same actions; a different place; the woman's head towards Isabella this time, the man astride the body so she could see his face ... the face of Kenneth Mackenzie. Now her way was clear. She must rid the world of this evil man ... now! Before he could do further damage. Soon, at the full moon, he would strike again somewhere else, many miles from the castle. If she didn't go at once he wouldn't be there. But she had very little time. A quick glance at the paper showed there were only three nights until the full moon. Tonight then. Tonight she must go home and tomorrow evening - night - the deed must be done. Only she knew what to do to prevent more murders; more assaults. She knew exactly how it was to be done. By burning. A twentieth century seer (and murderer) would meet his own death at the hands of the woman he had wronged. As it had happened three centuries before so it would happen again.

More because she had to have somewhere to hand where she could be sick in a hurry, than because she had any hope of sleeping, she reserved herself a first-class sleeper. At least she would be able to make plans without interruption and these were vital. No one must see her; no one must suspect. Nothing must go wrong. A fleeting idea of going to the police she dismissed almost immediately. They'd never believe her and the whole ignoble tale would in a very short while become public knowledge, since she was by no means sure she could successfully suppress her part in it. Nor did she think her 'magic' would constitute satisfactory proof of two murders. And the scandal. She couldn't ... she simply couldn't do this to Alison, Angus and all the others. Trying to put that aspect of the business out of her head, she went out and bought with her saved-up clothing coupons a Burberry mackintosh, a large headscarf of fine wool and a pair of crepe-soled shoes. She also cashed a cheque for £100.

Arriving at Inverness, she reserved a sleeper for the following night back to London. Without waiting for breakfast she went straight to the bus station, found she had just time to consult the timetable and make a note of the two buses she would need the services of over the next day and night, and caught another on the point of leaving for Fraserburgh on the East Coast.

It meandered along the coast road stopping at the least excuse to pick up or set down a passenger, whether there was an official stop or not. Isabella sat gazing out of the window over the Moray Firth thinking that somewhere over there, where the shores of the Black Isle drop away and vanish into mist, was the place where the other Seer had met his death - in a blazing tar barrel with spikes set pointing inwards. And he had screamed ... how he had screamed. Both she and the other Isabella who had lived three centuries before her - both of them had heard him. Would Kenneth Mackenzie scream, she wondered. In spite of everything, she rather hoped not, even though she would not be there to hear him. In any case, she suddenly realised a slight chill feeling sliding up her spine, she would know. She had the Stone. She couldn't help knowing.

At Nairn she felt safe enough to get off the bus and find somewhere for lunch. After that, she would walk on the shore finalising her plans until it was time to catch a returning bus to Inverness and then when it was quite dark, another to

Cononbridge. It was a nuisance having to come all this way, but even though she had only been at the castle for eight months and hardly ever came to Inverness, there was a chance someone might see her in Inverness and recognise her ... tell Angus or Alison. And perchance ... the thought caused a sharp shudder to run through her ... she might run into Mackenzie himself. Which was why she was going to stick to buses. She had never needed their services before. Always she had gone by train or with Angus and Alison in the car on their rare visits when there was enough petrol for a shopping jaunt to Inverness.

She walked on the beach all afternoon and by the time she got back to Inverness it was almost dark. Waiting at the bus station she pulled up the collar of the Burberry and tied the scarf over her hair. It was as good a disguise as any.

The walk from the bus stop at Cononbridge to the castle normally took about an hour taken at a good strapping pace. Tonight it took rather longer. It was pitch dark with a rising wind, but it was safer for her than moonlight. Even so, whenever a car passed - three or four only - she took care to step into the shadows well out of range of their headlights.

It would have been quicker and safer in one way to go up the drive, but to get to the castle she would have to pass the keeper's lodge and the dogs would bark.

Once at home, arrived at by carrying on past the lodge with its welcoming lights where Angus and Alison were probably now having their tea, she slipped through the fence and walked down through the field. She let herself in and paused for a moment, fumbling for the light switch. Then she suddenly remembered. No lights. She must make do with candles and be careful not to show them at any of the windows.

The house was very cold, damp and dark with the cheerless feeling of desertion that comes over a house of that kind the minute it is left on its own. It didn't take long for

Isabella to find herself a light. All over the house candlesticks were stationed at frequent intervals, each with a box of damp matches at hand. She found some now, using three before she could light one of the candles in the library, a room whose windows looked only west and were therefore invisible to anyone not actually in the courtyard at the time. She sat down on a red leather chair and wondered what to do for the next few hours. She was tired and would have liked to lie on her bed, but she was afraid of going to sleep. And her plans for the incineration of Kenneth Mackenzie weren't so elaborate after all. A small hurricane lamp, a torch for herself, a stump of candle and a small container full of paraffin.

It was a long wait in the dark, cold house with only a candle and small scuffling sounds for company. She sat for a while listening for the sonorous whirr of the big clock, meaning it was about to strike. At eight o'clock she wandered into her little kitchen and lit two more candles. Here she was safe. It was only a large cupboard with a skylight and, like the library, was on the west side. She drank some water, found a tin of baked beans and ate them cold with a spoon. This not very encouraging meal finished she collected together the things she would need and sat down again on a hard kitchen chair, longing for the business to be completed so she could go back to London again and complete <u>that</u> business, too. And as quickly as possible. She wondered what Keith - Dr. Mackenzie - would have to do for it to be possible. Not the physical aspect of it. She already knew as much as she wanted to about <u>that</u> - but an abortion was illegal. Perhaps he'd have to certify her as mad - which shouldn't be too difficult if deliberately creeping off in the middle of the night to burn someone's house (preferably with them in it) could be considered as qualifying. She grew colder and colder and very sleepy. She thought drowsily about Keith - Dr. Mackenzie, she corrected herself. She liked him.

Surprisingly he seemed to like her. And he was easy to talk to; reassuring; comfortable. It would be really rather nice to see him again, even under her pitiful circumstances. She hoped ... she dozed off and only saved herself from falling off her chair by a sudden clutch at the door-handle which woke her up completely. Half past ten. Time to go.

She put the torch in her pocket, the end of a candle. The hurricane lamp ... full; the container of paraffin tightly screwed up, and a dry box of matches which went into an oilskin bag and that was all.

She found her bicycle where she had left it ... paused for a moment, then decided not to take it. If for some reason she had to leave it there, that would be her cover blown completely.

She locked the door and put the key under its usual piece of broken slate. She walked up the drive towards the stables, the little hurricane lamp swinging from her hand, turned left at the stables and started off down the west drive. Half way down there was a path which led out onto the road and directly opposite was the track leading to the loch.

It was a wild night but the clouds whirling hurriedly across the sky were broken, and every so often the moon broke through, lighting her path. It was a good night for her purpose. The wind would muffle her approach, though lighting the hurricane lamp might be difficult.

At the croft there was no sign of life. Isabella crept along the grass by the path, her rubber-soled shoes making no sound. The success of her enterprise depended on two things; one was that Kenneth would be in bed, too drunk to hear any odd noises; the other on her being able to get into the house at all. This didn't worry her. Nobody ever locked their doors except at night, nor were afraid to leave croft or ground floor windows open even at night. Especially not here. No one, except Angus, and he as rarely as possible, ever came near the place. Had he thought about it at all, Kenneth would have imagined himself as safe.

There were no windows open but the front door wasn't locked. Isabella pushed it open very carefully, stuck her head in and listened. She would have liked some drunken snores but all she could hear was the wind. She pushed it open a little further and went cautiously in. She paused. Still no sound. Very, very carefully she silently walked across the room and towards the kitchen which gave on to the yard - and the west. She paused and listened again ... imagined she heard snores, but still heard only the wind. She shut the inner door and quickly tried the outer door of the kitchen for a speedy getaway; shut it again and knelt down on the floor to light the hurricane lamp and the stump of candle, shielding the match with her hand. Now, the lamp once lit, she must be quick. She put it down on the floor beside her, unscrewed the container and poured some of the contents over the mangy coconut mat which stood before the grease-encrusted gas cooker. She half screwed the stopper of the hurricane lamp back on and laid the lamp on its side near the window. The paraffin began to leak slowly out of the base of the little lamp, making its way in a dusty trail towards the mat. She lifted up the edge of the mat, held the candle flame over to it, taking care not to let drips fall onto the floor and waited for a moment until it was well ablaze. It took no time; too little. She jumped up and back as the flames surged up from the grease-soaked mat, and half opened the window. The wind leapt in causing the flames to flatten and writhe like the waves of the sea. But they were too well established for the wind to extinguish them now. Isabella took a quick last look to make sure there was nothing incriminating left behind, opened the kitchen door and sped silently away.

A while later Miss Phemie Macdonald, the postmistress

of the little clachan, awakened by the insistent calls of her cat to be allowed to come in out of the rain, saw a red glow on the other side of the loch. She watched it for a few moments undecided, but it didn't seem to be making much progress - rather the glow seemed to be diminishing. She let in the cat and waited a bit longer. The fire was definitely dying down. No need to call the fire brigade then. She addressed the cat in scornful tones. "Nae wonder he's let the place catch on fire, the wicked, heathen, drunken body. Och weel, this rain'll soon pit it oot. Guid riddance to him, I say. Come awa' ben Tibbles," and picking up the wet cat she went back to bed. She'd often wondered what had happened to Tibbles the first. Let out one night - the night of the full moon - he never came back. And she'd heard tales ... She blew out her candle and on the other side of the loch the fire expired in hissing steam.

Later still the setting moon looking in at Isabella's window shone palely upon her upturned face as she lay on her bed, half dressed, under a mound of blankets; only a short while since she had stopped shivering and fallen into an exhausted sleep.

She slept till noon, then got up and ate another tin of cold baked beans; decided she didn't care if she never saw another baked bean in her life; drank some water and then went out to dispose of the two empty tins where Alison, preparing for her return, would not see them. "I'm getting rather good at deceit," she thought wearily. She yawned, pushed her hair away from her forehead and went back into the castle to wait. Remembered the spoons; washed them and the glass, put them both away and sat down again. None of this had taken very long but she must wait until it was properly dark before she could leave - which was the one thing she didn't want to do - ever again. It would take all her resolution to make her leave her beloved home, possibly never to see it again. If only she could stay here and deal with things in her own way, with a knitting needle, if that was really what they used. Then she thought of Alison's distress and she pulled herself together with a jerk.

Darkness comes early to the Highlands towards the end of October though it still wanted a week before the clocks went back. The bus wasn't due until six but it would be better to start walking to Inverness rather than stay here becoming colder and colder and more faint-hearted by the second. At five she was ready; quite clean and tidy considering her adventure. She went into the drawing-room to take leave of Isabella, as though by so doing she could ensure that the second of the two seers who had so sorely troubled these two women, three hundred years apart in time, should himself suffer a meet penalty. It was too dark to see the portrait so she stood for a moment under it, said: "I'll be back soon; wish me luck in my venture," and let herself quietly out. She replaced the key under the slate and started off up the hill for the second time in twenty-four hours.

At about the same time as Isabella set out on the last leg of her journey, Kenneth Mackenzie, getting off the train at Inverness where he had come from a sale of agricultural equipment in Perth, was about to do the same - in his little van.

He had planned on reaching Inverness to go and drink in a pub somewhere where he had never been before and then head for a brothel. It would have to be a familiar one because there were only two in Inverness and he had often visited both. But in the pub he changed his mind. There was something about brothels now which made him uneasy. It was to do with the well-remembered feeling of his hands round a woman's neck (probably in his subconscious mind the neck belonged to

102

Isabella, who would never now know what a lucky escape she had had on that horrible afternoon). The urge to kill was present again tonight, the night of the full moon, but it did not seem as strong as on the last two occasions. He didn't feel as virile as usual either, and after he had sat as long as he could in the pub, until the landlord had practically to throw him out, he lurched into the road, much drunker than he realised, considering he'd got through the evening mostly on beer. He found his way into the driving seat and decided he couldn't be bothered with the whores tonight. He'd go home where there was a new bottle of whisky waiting to be opened. He'd get properly soused, which a man couldn't on this mixture of bath salts and disinfectant which passed for beer nowadays. After that, if he felt like it, he'd go out and strangle Miss Macdonald's new cat. With this agreeable programme in mind he drove to the edge of the town, was suddenly seized by a huge yawn, pulled into the side of the road and fell asleep.

He slept for three hours and woke feeling less tired, but still not inclined to look for a whore. He started up the engine and with his foot flat to the floor drove as fast as the old van could rattle. He could feel the nervous shaking and twitchings and the beginnings of a cold sweat; familiar symptoms to him after he'd gone without whisky for long. He must hurry to his bottle. Now he was beginning to feel really bad. Squeakily bouncing and vibrating, the ancient vehicle tore along the road, and with only one headlamp functioning came to the Clachnaharry railway bridge sooner than anticipated. Just beyond the village there was the sign indicating an almost right-angled turn across the bridge, and another on the left verge was also there, but the one headlamp, skimming the outer edge, missed it. He wrenched the car round, got it across the bridge, but failed to negotiate the tight, left-hand bend which would bring him back on to the stretch of straight road which runs along the foreshore of the Beauly Firth.

Back in London, filling in the time until her next appointment on the following day by going to see 'Gone With The Wind' for the fourth time, Isabella was puzzled for, the previous night on the train, the 'seeing' had taken a completely new form from what she had expected and known before.

In her state of mind and still tired by her mission (which she was beginning to think of as a damp squib - the croft had felt so empty) it would not have been surprising if she had been treated to a complete rehash - 20th Century Fox; period costumes; tortured screams and all - of the original Burning. This time there were no screams for which she was thankful beyond measure. There was no noise at all. She was in a small boat, 'seeing' from the water instead of the land; the sea. She recognised over her shoulder the low outline of the Black Isle, vague in the dark and the long arm of land close to her left leading to the jetty where the Kessock ferry plied to and fro across the Firth. But it was a split second's glimpse, no more, for suddenly something came hurtling over the low parapet bordering the main Inverness road to the north and west. A car - a small van - landed on the foreshore, very close, and a huge ball of orange fire billowed up, completely engulfing the vehicle. This time, instead of fading and returning like the previous 'seeings' the picture cut out abruptly and did not return.

She was still puzzling over it and on her way to her appointment next day was impelled to buy a paper from a small newsagent in Wigmore Street, hoping that it would be able to throw some light on this, so far the most prophetic of her seeings. She was also puzzled by the Stone. It had changed since she got it back. Now it no longer took her back to the distant past (perhaps she had to be at home for it to do that) but seemed concerned with the present or very recent past.

Thus the two women on the derelict pieces of land with Mackenzie's hands round their throats, and now the car or van landing on the foreshore and catching fire. "Fire!" had cried the Seer; "I see the fire!" And this ... this fire too, she was certain, had to do with Kenneth Mackenzie (though totally unconnected with her attempted burning of his croft). Nothing to do with her at all, if it was what she thought - that he had been in the middle of that huge billowing ball of fire. No wonder there had been no screams. There wouldn't have been time. She would find out - or rather hear about it, if it was to do with him, sooner or later. For reasons of her own, she was certainly not going to make any enquiries, she thought, as she got off the bus and made her way up Wimpole Street.

To her considerable disappointment, when she was shown into the consulting-room another man stood behind Keith. A much older man, tall and thin with a pursed up mouth, wearing a dark suit and a peevish expression; he looked at her without smiling. Hesitating on the threshold, she must have shown her feelings plainly for Keith came round from behind his desk and said, "This is Mr. Guthrie, Miss Mackenzie. He may be able to help you." The man came forward and offered Isabella his hand. She took it reluctantly.

"But ... but I thought ... I mean, why do I have to see someone else ... as well?" she asked. "I've told you all I can. I've told you the truth. There's nothing more to say, surely ... " she added rather desperately. "If you don't believe me, say so now and I'll ... I'll go. I don't want any fuss. I'd ... I'd rather do it on my own ... "

"Sit down, Miss Mackenzie," said Keith, gently. He put a hand on her shoulder and applied a little pressure. Obediently she sat down but stayed perched on the edge of the chair, looking very mulish. Immediately she sensed that this Guthrie person didn't like her. He wouldn't help her. Why had Keith dragged him into it, just as they were getting on so well? It was too bad of him. Now she'd have to go through the whole awful story all over again. She felt let down, defeated and thoroughly miserable.

"Mr. Guthrie's a surgeon, Miss Mackenzie," said Keith gently. "I'm only a consultant. I'm not able to do operations. And we must go along with the rules, you know. It is absolutely necessary for a second opinion in a case like this. I promise we won't make things more difficult for you than we can help. Now Mr. Guthrie must ask you a few questions. Nothing much. He knows the facts already."

"Ay," said the surgeon, looking at her keenly. "Dr. Mackenzie tells me ye've been the victim of an assault as a result of which ye're now aboot ten weeks pregnant. But ye see it's a wee bit deeficult. In order to use this as a reason for terminating your pregnancy on sich grounds we need a conviction. Which means ye'd have to appear in court and testify. Anither deeficulty; it appears ye offered a wheen provocation."

"If you call what I did provocation ... " began Isabella hotly, but was silenced by a tiny shake of the head from Keith standing a little behind the other man and to one side, where he could not be seen except by the girl.

"Na, na; maybe I wouldna' but the Court might," said the surgeon, his voice implying that of course he did too. "It's a possibility we canna' discount. Dr. Mackenzie tells me ye had considered marrying the man to gie the bairn a father. Could ye no do that? It might work out."

"The man's a murderer," Isabella said flatly. "Was, I mean. I think he's dead." The two men looked at each other, startled.

"What?" exclaimed Keith. "But the last time ... um, well you said nothing about this."

"It hadn't happened then. But now I know he's a murderer and I'll soon know if he's dead. I'm almost sure he is, but as he's one of my tenants, Angus, my factor, will let me know."

"A murderer?" asked Guthrie. "But that's a very serious charge ye're making, young lady."

Keith interrupted. There was a slight edge to his voice: "I'm sure Miss Mackenzie is well aware of the seriousness of her allegation, Mr. Guthrie," he said with asperity; "and that she would not say such a thing without good reason."

"Ay, if ye say so. But ye say ye ken for sairtain the man's a murderer? Hoo do ye ken this?"

"I saw it happening," said Isabella sulkily, well aware how ridiculous it must sound, and of the total impossibility of being believed by either of them. "It was on waste land in two different places and he had his hands round one woman's neck ... I couldn't see the other - he had his back to me - but the one I <u>did</u> see was facing me and ... well, after he'd, I suppose, strangled her, he took something out of his pocket and sort of drew it round her neck under her chin ... from one ear to the other, and each time there was a full moon."

"And ye actually saw this happening?" asked Guthrie with incredulity. "Ye were <u>there</u>? I canna credit it. And were ye no shocked and horrified at sich a thing? And ye didna tell the Polus?"

"No, I wasn't actually there. And of course I ... it was ... well, a sort of dream, if you like ... except it wasn't a dream. It was more of a vision. Unreal, except that it was ... could have been ... I've had them before. I had one two nights ago. It was a great ball of fire ... a car, I imagine ... or a van. It came over the parapet and onto the foreshore and burst into flames. And I <u>think</u> that man was in it. I hope so."

The surgeon seemed bereft of words. Aware that Keith was looking keenly at her, she turned to him imploringly.

"I haven't made it up, I promise. It was the Stone."

Again Keith very slightly shook his head.

"Sich a tale ... " said the surgeon with enormous disapproval. " - well Doctor, I havena' a'; the time in the world. We'd best be getting on wi' it."

"Getting on with what?" asked Isabella in alarm.

"Just a small examination," said Keith soothingly. "Mr. Guthrie has to satisfy himself on certain points. It won't take long, but we can't go any further without it. It seems a shame after all you have had to put up with, but I promise you it is absolutely necessary. Nurse?"

It was too much. She could bear no more. She lay with her eyes tightly shut, once more clutching the pink blanket to her chin as the surgeon proceeded with yet another exploration of her poor, violated, humiliated body. And these hands were not gentle like Doctor Mackenzie's. These were the hands of a butcher rummaging inside a carcass, hurting her deliberately because she was a fallen woman. Two large tears escaped and rolled silently down her sad, pale face. A hand, warm and friendly, reached across the blanket, found one of hers and held it tightly. She opened her eyes, thinking it was the nurse who sympathised with her after all, and saw Keith (for a brief moment no longer the doctor) smiling down at her, taking no part in the examination. She shut her eyes again quickly, embarrassed by her show of weakness, but a little comforted. Then at last she was free. She dressed wearily and went with lagging steps back to the consulting-room. The surgeon, looking grim, was preparing to leave.

"If you're not in too much of a hurry, Miss Mackenzie," said Keith smoothly, "would you mind waiting a moment longer?" I've just got a word or two to say to Mr. Guthrie. I won't be long."

She went and sat in the waiting-room, staring out of the window at the traffic going past and the pigeons perched on the roof of the house opposite. The door opened and Keith

108

came in.

"Well, we're rid of him, thank goodness," he said cheerfully. "He's being awfully piggy; you know ... John Knox ..."

"... and fallen women," put in Isabella quickly.

"Well, yes. But he would, of course. Never mind. I think I'll be able to talk him round. But what I came to ask you was, if you're not doing anything with anybody in particular, would you have dinner with me sometime? Tonight, if possible. I've got my hospital consultancy now, but I'll be free by seven. Could you? Can you? We've got a lot to talk about I feel. Do say yes."

The blood rushed to her face.

"Oh ... oh, yes. How kind of you ... " she stammered. "Tonight would be lovely."

"Well I'll call for you at half past seven. The Eaton Hotel, isn't it? Come on. It's on my way; I'll give you a lift."

Oh, thought Isabella as they sped through the streets in Keith's sleek, black Bentley Tourer. He is so _nice_. I know he's only being kind to me because he's sorry for me, but this is _wonderful_. Now ... in this heavenly car and with a whole evening with him to look forward to.

They talked of nothings during the drive, which was over much too quickly. But as he drove away, looking back for a second over his shoulder to wave, he saw her standing on the step, one of her rare, happy smiles on her thin face and he thought, 'I wonder. If ever I heard a more rum tale. I wonder _very_ much.' Highland by blood, he decided to put medical scepticism away for the evening - he'd had enough of it from Guthrie for one day. He'd go along with Isabella. He was beginning to rather like her. Poor little thing. A sad tale; a rotten upbringing; and after a private conversation with her, he'd be in a much better position with old Guthrie. He found he was looking forward to it. And his determination to help her was intensified when a patient who had tried a self-inflicted abortion was brought in beyond his or anyone's help, and would probably die that night.

There was a message for Isabella at the reception desk. To ring the Estate Office. She ran to the telephone box, dialled and asked for Trunks. It took a little while to get through. Then she heard Angus's voice, rather faint but clear.

"Is that you, Miss Bella? Guid. I asked ye to ring me as I've a wee bit news for ye. Consairning our Kenneth. Can ye hear me?"

"Yes, yes. Go on."

"Well, it seems that there's been a fire at the croft and he's no there the noo, and hasna' been seen by anyin for twa days. It appears the fire was started by a wee lamp - a hurricane lamp which it appears he must hae left lichtit on the windowsill and the wind blew it over. The paraffin must hae leekit oot and that's hoo they believe it starrted."

"Is it ... I mean ... is the croft completely destroyed?" asked Isabella, trying to sound convincingly surprised.

"Nae quite. But it's no habitable."

"But he wasn't there?"

"Na. But there's a funny thing, Miss Bella. The Polus are after me. They're wishfu' to identify some remains ... "

"Remains? Do you mean of ... of a body, Angus?"

"Ay. It's no offeecial news yet, but it appears that a wee cawr ... a van ... went ower the parapet at the bridge at Clachnaharry ... ye ken the place ... where ye maun turn sharrp richt and then left almost immediately? Aweel, this laddie didna' turrn left but went straight on and syne landit up on the foreshore. Seemingly the van caught on fire and was near burnt oot when the tide came in."

"And they think it's Kenneth Mackenzie?"

"Ay," said Angus, sounding a bit surprised. "Did ye ken, Miss Bella? Have ye hearrd anything ... ?"

"No, no. Nothing. I just had a feeling."

"I speir it's yon stane," said Angus with a small, rumbling laugh.

"Perhaps. When did this all happen?"

"Yesterrday morrning. In the wee sma' hours. They had to bide until the tide went oot as the van was part under the water so they didna' get him oot until late last evening. I went to the mortuary earrly this morning to identify the laddie ... sic as was left of him. I kenned him by his trews and there wasna' muckle left of them either, but the wee van still had its number plates. It'll a' be in the papers tomorrow."

"Oh, Angus. Could you be a dear and send me some cuttings? It may not be in the London papers and I ... well ... I need to convince someone of something. I'll tell you all about it one day."

"Ay, I'll do that, Miss Bella. Alison and me we've kenned it a' a lang whiles syne and we're unco' sorry for ye. It doesna' do to speak ill of the deid, but I'm muckle glad he'll no trouble us furrther."

"Oh, so am I," said Isabella fervently. 'And not to be a murderess either,' she thought, sanity having in some slight measure returned to her. She felt suddenly very cold 'I must have been mad, trying to burn him alive.'

"Are ye still there, Miss Bella?" asked Angus anxiously.

"Yes. How's Alison?"

"Och, she's fine. And sends her dear love. But ... I dinna ken if I ought to tell ye, but there's something ither ... "

"To do with Kenneth?"

"Ay. It seems - unoffeecially, ye ken - that the Polus was after oor laddie in connection with twa murrders. Yin in Glesga, the ither in Dundee. Twa ... er ... weemen o' the streets."

"Oh, Angus," she said sighing heavily. "I know about that too. I 'saw' him murder them both. And I 'saw' the car come over the parapet." She hadn't meant to tell him, but as he knew all about her already in spite of her efforts to hide her troubles from them both, it was an enormous relief not to have to hide anything from these two, her two dear friends. Keith she could tell, though he might not ... probably wouldn't ... believe her, but that didn't matter. It mattered enormously that she should have no secrets from either Angus or Alison Stewart. She owed it to them.

She looked towards the door where the page boy was gibbering at her through the window. "He's here," she thought, exultant. "Dear Angus," she said. "Don't worry. It's all been horrid, but everything should be alright now."

"But ... but are ye a'richt yersel', Miss Bella? I mean ... "

"I'm quite alright, Angus dear. Really. And I'll be home soon. Please don't worry. You must be tired. Have an early night. Love to Alison and promise not to worry about me, tell her."

"If ye say so. Guid nicht then, Miss Bella and come ye hame soon. We a' miss ye."

Bless him, she thought, ringing off. If only I could. What a trouble I've been to them. But never again. I'm grown-up now. Things will be very different when I do get home.

Keith, waiting for her in the hall, thought, as had Wotherspoon the younger, 'My God'. But not 'how ugly she is'. He saw a tall, slight figure dressed in a simple tartan wool dress with a reverse collar, long sleeves and a finely all-round pleated skirt. Silver buttons from an old uniform of an officer of the Seaforth Highlanders; her caberfeidh brooch; a severe black belt; black court shoes and a black velvet ribbon band to keep back her hair. Little make-up, except for brown mascara for eyebrows and eyelashes and only the faintest trace of lipstick.

112

That was Isabella - a very different person from the sad figure on his consulting-room couch earlier in the afternoon.

He thought again, 'My God'. Style; distinction; she's got them both. She's special.'

They shook hands formally and she offered him a drink. He drank a small whisky and soda in the hotel lounge and then he bore her off in the Bentley, parked just up the street, to a restaurant of his own finding where they could be sure of being neither hurried, overheard, nor interrupted.

She couldn't drink ordinary wine because it made her sick so he ordered a bottle of Moët et Chandon and a simple dinner which wouldn't upset her next day.

"Now," he said, "the feast is ordered and my ears are yours to command. First of all I must apologise for grimacing at you in that highly unprofessional way this afternoon, but I thought that if you were to try and tell the old porpoise about your stone, he'd take it from you and throw it at you while watching you burn at the stake." But she did not smile. She said:

"He is like the Black Priest," quite seriously.

"The Black Priest?"

"That prating, capering, treacherous cleric," she quoted sombrely. "That's what she called him - Isabella. He took the Stone from the Seer before he was thrown into the barrel of blazing tar. He shouldn't have done that. But it didn't work for him anymore than it did for her. I'm glad."

"You didn't like him much, old Guthrie ... did you?"

"He didn't like me at all. He thinks I'm a fallen woman; he didn't trouble to hide it."

"Perhaps he sensed something about you he couldn't understand. He doesn't like anything that isn't clear-cut medically. But bear with him. He's a wonderful surgeon and this business can be tricky. You don't want to be messed up so

113

you can never have an heir, do you?" She shook her head slowly and fell silent. After a moment, watching her playing with a bit of bread, he asked rather curiously: "Will you show me your stone?"

"Of course." She slipped the ribbon over her head, untied the one holding the neck of the little bag together and slid the Stone onto his hand.

"Would it work for me, do you think?" he asked. "May I keep it for a moment?"

"Yes. I can manage without it nowadays ... though not for too long. In fact ... I'm not sure ... but it's all different now. It's power has changed. Keith," she said suddenly, leaning towards him, her expression very serious and quite unaware, he decided, that she had used his Christian name ... "do you think that ... um ... Kenneth Mackenzie ... has somehow contaminated it? He was such a horrible person. Could he have somehow transferred his own evil powers to it ... which are stronger than its own? Whatever they are."

He looked at it as it lay in his hand.

"It doesn't really seem as though anything as small as this would have much in the way of occult powers - let alone the ability to cause the harm you say it has done. Do you really believe that this man, Mackenzie ... and I wonder if his name really <u>was</u> Mackenzie ... is a murderer? And do you think of him as a descendant of the Seer? I suppose he must be connected in some way, or the stone would not have worked for him as you say it did. And he's <u>dead</u>, you say?"

Isabella told him of her conversation with Angus.

"We've only got to wait for the newspaper cuttings to prove it."

"Well, I'll be blowed. And you 'saw' ... well, anticipated ... all this?"

She nodded.

114

"Would I be able to ... being a Mackenzie?"

"Oh, don't try. It's awful; not nice a bit; nobody likes people like us who are different. It's most uncomfortable being a seer. Our knowledge, like the Raven's, sets us apart."

"And what is that knowledge?"

"Oh ... of 'seeing' things and happenings that are best left unseen. And ... of hurting too."

"Have the 'seeings' been going on for long," asked Keith, seeking for a possible medical explanation.

"The actual 'seeing' ... no. For only a week. The other times I only heard and because I was a bit alarmed I tended to hide under the bedclothes ... especially on the night of the screams, I'm afraid. But it was all so real and I know I was awake. There was so much noise. Horses neighing; people ... men ... in great boots tramping up and down the passage outside the door of my room. Laughing; shouting; singing ... that's how I knew ... because it was his voice singing. It couldn't possibly have been a dream; nor could the screams. And the way it kept fading and returning until it had vanished completely ... I couldn't have imagined all that ... or could I? I simply don't know."

"Could it have been something to do with the room?"

"It could, I suppose. But I'd been in that room for a while without hearing anything ... until I found the Stone."

"What makes you think that the stone is a power for good? If it is indeed the real one, it seems to me that if it has any power at all, it is mostly for harm. I wonder if Mackenzie murdered anyone before he took the stone from you. Whichever, it certainly doesn't seem to have done him much good."

"It did me ... at first. I sort of came alive. And I was tremendously happy, which I'd never been before. As long as I had it with me. But if I was without it for any length of time, I felt ... well, sort of desolate, I suppose one could say."

115

"Well, Isabella Mackenzie, I don't want to detract from your Stone's supernatural powers because I believe such things are possible and exist. But the fact remains, as a follower of scientific theory, I don't think these things ... neither the visions nor the hearings would happen to someone who didn't possess a certain object, whether it's a stone or a dried cow's tail supposedly blessed by a witch. Or a garter of plaited rushes made by the fairy Mélusine and worn as a talisman round the elbow and bringing good luck, if not actual immortality, to its owner. Personally I'd prefer a stone. A cow's tail might be rather smelly, and a rush bracelet or garter, whatever it was, would be very scratchy to wear. What say you?"

She laughed, liking both the teasing and the original form of address, not too intimate for such a brief acquaintance and not too formal either.

"But surely that's just the point. Kenneth Mackenzie as far as we know, didn't commit any murders until he had the Stone ... not human murders, that is. But I think ... Angus wouldn't tell me ... but I think he'd killed some animals; he'd been fined for cruelty to them. And there was that dog ... " She told him about the dog and her conviction.

"Even so. It's not the so-called magic object that causes these things to happen. The power isn't in the object ... it's in the person. Once they've got hold of it they and other people eventually become convinced of their magic powers and they are sufficiently bewitched; taken-in; credulous ... anything you like, for it to become a strong influence, even an obsession; and sometimes it takes them over completely, and that's when there's trouble."

But she shook her head seriously, not believing him. He watched her, amused by her expression.

"Then how do you account for the murders?" she asked.

"If he really did them, then I'd say the stone gave him the

idea, or the courage, to do something he'd have done sooner or later anyway, stone or no stone," he said, thinking, 'and it could so easily have been you'. "The man was a dangerous psychopath who ought to have been put behind bars years ago. Thank goodness this happened before he could do you any more harm. I don't somehow think you'd have felt too secure at the castle after everything, with him still at large."

"I should have had to marry him," said Isabella sombrely. "To avoid a scandal ... if I couldn't ... well, you know.   It doesn't solve anything ... if I can't ... "

"Get rid of the baby, you mean? Oh, my God." He rose and put a large number of pound notes on top of the bill. "We must go."

At the hotel he drew up a little way beyond the door and as she held out her hand, beginning to thank him, he said:

"Don't. It's been my pleasure and most interesting. Now don't expect to hear from me for a few days because I've got to go to Edinburgh. I'll only be away until Tuesday. I mean, I'll be in London again on Tuesday and I'll have an answer for you. The best of it is that the Black Priest is going to the same conference and he'll see the whole thing in the Scottish newspapers so he can't help but believe - if it is all as you say it is. I, for one do. Anyway, he'll be completely convinced and we'll have no more trouble with him, though of course he'll come up with a convincing medical explanation if he possibly can. Even if a corpse climbed off the mortuary slab and shook its fist at him, he'd come up with a medical explanation sooner or later. But not even he could want you to carry on with this now. Another thing; he'll have all the fun of telling anyone who will listen ... bore the trews off them, knowing him ... that he once had a patient who had the second sight. I pity his poor family, I do really. Now don't worry. All will be well. <u>And</u> ... listen to me, Isabella Mackenzie, when I return I want - not only to see you looking as least as chirpy as you've been this evening - but to have once more the pleasure of your company. So we'll plan another dinner, shall we? Soon?" And Isabella, who had sat very silent while he spoke, thinking what an awfully long time it was until she should see him again, cheered up wonderfully.

He got out and opened the door for her. She held out her hand. He took it, then patted it.

"Goodbye," he said. "Same time Tuesday? Good. Look after your little self." He waved as he drove away.

Angus did not fail her. The letter from him containing a cutting from the local paper arrived on Monday morning. It contained all she needed:

> The remains of a man found in a partly burnt-out van on the foreshore of the Beauly Firth at Clachnaharry have been identified as those of Kenneth Mackenzie, 30. The Commer van is believed to have left the road and gone over the parapet at the notorious accident spot of Clachnaharry Bridge in the early hours of Wednesday morning when Mr.. Mackenzie was returning home to his rented croft, which was partly destroyed by fire two days before. The cause of the fire is thought to be a lighted hurricane lantern placed on the windowsill and blown onto the floor. The deceased, who was absent at the time, was being sought by the Police for questioning in connection with the recent murders of two women in Glasgow in August and Dundee last month. Mr. Mackenzie had the reputation of being a heavy drinker and had a previous conviction for cruelty to animals.

It was as brief as possible. The Editor of this particular

paper did not care for this sort of news. He prided himself, at a time when he saw decent Christian values being eroded all round him, on the high moral tone of the events and sentiments he permitted to be recorded. But it was all that Isabella needed. She put it carefully in her shoulder bag and went off to the Zoo.

She had dinner with Keith on Tuesday. All was well, he informed her. He had made the necessary arrangements and she was to report to an address in Welbeck Street, a small nursing home the following day. The operation would take place on Thursday morning and she would probably be able to go home on Monday. He'd seen both the report in the paper and he'd seen the Black Priest in Edinburgh, who had almost burst himself endeavouring not to be impressed by her visions. "Oh, he tried," said Keith laughing. "How he tried; but he couldn't come up with any explanations. I quoted Hamlet at him and finally he mumbled something about it being a 'coeencidence'; gave me a look of great dislike; warned me not to encourage you in these 'havers' and went away. But he was having a fine time for all that, telling people. He kept looking at me, and then turning back to them, talking with great earnestness, and I could see that they were one and all rootling about in their great brains also trying to come up with explanations and failing. What an old hypocrite he is. I'm sure he believes in the second sight as much as anyone, but would rather be burnt at the stake than admit it. Goes against his Knoxian principles. All the same, it is odd. You must admit it."

Isabella did, but without much conviction. Already it was something she was learning to live with, like her skua's nose and sandy eyebrows and lashes. As long as the 'seeings' remained within reasonable bounds, she supposed she could live with them.

119

The operation went well, but the resulting haemorrhage was severe. It persisted for several days, leaving her weak and very depressed. Keith was there when she surfaced and came every evening to see her, bringing books and flowers and things to eat. She liked his visits and looked forward to them, but she was too tired to talk much. She hadn't realised she would feel so, well, almost bereaved. She had hated the very thought of the baby, but even when asked seriously by Keith if she wouldn't reconsider her decision and go through with it, she had been adamant. He had good cause to know what it would be like for her, whether she had wanted it or not. 'It is too fundamental a thing for them, poor creatures,' he thought sadly, 'for them to take it lightly. It's not after all like having a gall bladder or an appendix removed.'

She cried a great deal, though she tried to hide it. Keith thought she would be better at home now and after a week, when the bleeding had stopped, he booked a sleeper for her on the night train (having forewarned Angus) and drove her to the station. They had dinner at the Euston Hotel and she tried very hard to be cheerful. It was difficult. She didn't know if she would ever see him again. Now, with parting imminent, she realised how much she liked him and how easily she could come to depend on him. As he escorted her onto the train, found her sleeper for her and stowed away her luggage, she sat down on the bed with the feeling that her legs were giving away beneath her and said, rather shyly: "I can't thank you properly for all you've done for me, because there aren't enough of them ... ways of thanking you, I mean. If ... if you ever came to Scotland again ... for a fishing holiday, perhaps you'd ... you'd look in on me... I'd like to show you more of it than Angus had time for ... and we never really established our relationship, did we?" (Not in that respect, nor in any other," she thought sadly.)

"No. That must certainly be done without too much delay either? Thank you. I was afraid you weren't going to suggest it and then I would have had to be very forward and suggest it myself. As it is, all is well ... and it won't be long." The whistle blew. "I must go. Goodbye, Isabella Mackenzie, and remember, keep your feet up as much as possible until you feel stronger." He bent, kissed the top of her head lightly and quickly and was gone. She watched him walk away down the platform as the train, its wheels slipping a little, got snorting into its stride. Then she went back into her compartment and cried all the way to Nuneaton.

She stayed at home doing nothing very much for a week, tired and depressed; still weak from the loss of blood. Angus came every day to take her to lunch, because she didn't feel like walking. Once there Alison stuffed her with iron pills and excellent food and Angus would take her home at about three, refusing to leave her until he was sure she had enough wood to keep her fire going, without her having to trail up and down stairs carrying a heavy load.

She played the piano much of the time and in Inverness Angus bought the largest electric fire he could find which wouldn't blow the castle's precarious electrical system, for it was now November and very cold. Ben Wyvis was covered with snow, even its foothills, and it wouldn't be long before snow would cover the entire country.

One day at lunchtime Angus said:

"I'm thinking I must pay a wee veesit tae yon croft this afternoon, Miss Bella. I've reportit the fire to Mr. Wotherspoon, but I'd like it fine if ye wud come alang wi' me. I need yer advice."

"The ... the ... insurance?" asked Isabella very slowly.

"Aye. Mr. Wotherspoon will need to pit in a claim if we're tae rebuild."

"Rebuild? ... " faltered Isabella. This was something she hadn't thought of. It was one thing to burn down your own property (as long as there was nobody in it at the time) if you were so disposed, but to put in an insurance claim for the privilege didn't seem quite ethical, if, as she imagined, it meant getting money from the insurance company under false pretences. And yet, if they didn't claim, it would look most peculiar.

"Do go with Angus, dearie," urged Alison. "You'll be a help to him and he likes to have your company. He's been too long without anyone to take an interest. But ye mustn't let her stand about, Angus, and get cold and tired, mind."

Isabella assented, trying to sound a little more enthusiastic. Normally she liked going about with Angus visiting tenants, discussing improvements and innovations to be made when she should come into her inheritance properly ... but the croft ... that was different. Even without the question of the insurance claim, she had no desire ever to see the place again. Angus sensed her reluctance. In the car he said:

"I appreciate this, Miss Bella. It's no easy for ye to returrn to the place, but ye ken, I'm beginning to rely on ye for advice. This place has been ower lang wi' oot a laird. A' the worry fa's on the factor; not that I'm complaining, the estate's a'ways been my life, but it's a sair poseetion tae be in because I canna tak responsibility wi' oot the assent of Mr. Wotherspoon and what do the likes of him ken o' the needs of the crofters and tenants? I doot he's a fine lawyer, but he's no a country pairson, and there's a leemit to what he can sanction when it comes to spending money. That's why the place is in sic a sair state. Twa absentee landlords taking us back ower fifty years. Oo ay, I ken yer great-uncle was a sodger and a fine yin, but ye canna run a place like this frae India or the Colonies, Miss Bella. And ye've a fine brain and a guid thinking heid on ye. Ye're weel on the way tae making a braw laird."

Isabella was touched and put the recurring thought of Keith from her with some success.

The croft looked desolate, though some of it was untouched by fire - just black with smoke and utterly depressing. Isabella got out of the car, but instead of going in with Angus, who had a small notebook and pencil with him, she wandered round to the back which had been completely destroyed, though the westerly wind had blown the flames inward and left the outbuildings untouched. She opened a door, found herself in a biggish shed, came out at the other end and saw next to the privy another small lean-to shed with a broken door hanging crookedly from one hinge. She pulled it open. The light, a gleam of sun setting in the west, threw a beam onto a heap of something in the middle of the floor.

She bent down, looking more closely. There were bones - tiny, fragile, charred and blackened bones and some skulls. Small skulls, with here and there pathetic tufts of matted fur still sticking to them. She took a piece of wood from the corner and gently poked at the edge of the heap. The remains of a cat's tail emerged. She dropped the piece of wood in revulsion, backed hurriedly away and called out:

"Angus. Can you come here a minute?"

He appeared, and standing beside her rather grimly inspected the gruesome contents of the little shed. They studied them for a moment in silence.

"I know what this is," said Isabella suddenly. "It was in that book ... the one about the Seer. It's a way of predicting things. It's called 'taghairm'. It's from the ancient Druidic rites, when they roasted cats to help them to make a 'frith' or a spell or augur. It's black magic, I suppose. Satanism."

"So that's where Mistress Phemie Macdonald's puir pussy cat got to. An unco' weird customer, that Kenneth."

123

"Yes," said Isabella, shortly. "I'll go back and wait for you in the car, Angus."

He agreed. She looked white and tired. 'Puir lassie,' he thought. 'She's taking a long time recovering from whatever it was. And I wonder if yon doctor hasna' something tae do wi'it. A braw young man."

On the way home, Isabella brought up the subject of the ruined croft.

"If we put in a claim to the insurance company for rebuilding," she asked carefully, "will they pay out for the croft to be completely rebuilt or only for the bits which were destroyed?"

"I dinna ken," he answered. "That's up to Mr. Wotherspoon. He'll decide what's to be done, once I've sent him my report and the representative has ca'd."

"No, it isn't," she said decidedly. "Not altogether. You see, I don't think it should be rebuilt, or repaired at all. It's a bad place, Angus. A wicked, evil place. It ... it was <u>meant</u> to burn down and if we rebuild it, it will be unlucky for anyone who has to live in it."

"Verra likely, Miss Bella. But ye'll hae a muckle job pitting that opeenion tae Mr. Wotherspoon."

"We'll see," said Isabella. "But I won't have it rebuilt, that's all, whatever he says. It's to be demolished, and if the insurance company won't pay out, I'll pay for it myself. I've got a lot of money, Angus," she said, rather shyly as though aware the remark might be in bad taste. "My mother left me all hers. I don't need it. I shall ... yes, I know what I shall do. You know the McLennans, next to the ... the croft? Didn't you say Willie McLennan wanted a bit more land so he can graze some livestock? Well, we'll fence the croft off properly and Willie can have the land. The rest can be demolished and he can have what he wants of the outbuildings. You know, Angus, the way those poor McLennans live is a disgrace. Mrs. McLennan told me she has to get all the water from the well. They've no electricity ... "

"Naebody has the electricity, Miss Bella."

"We have. Occasionally."

Angus laughed. "Aye, but up the way they're right off the beaten track and what with the shortages of manpower and materials, they havena' yet been able to dae the worrk."

"Well, alright. We can't do anything about the electricity, but surely we can do something about running water? Couldn't we install an electric pump, working on batteries and connect it to the well or ... or something?" She looked at him enquiringly; her knowledge of such things was not extensive, but under Angus's tutelage was growing steadily, and she had been genuinely shocked at the condition under which Mrs. McLennan was trying to bring up three children as decently as she could.

"The well wad soon rin dry, I'm thinking. But there's the burrn. Aye, yer richt. We could divert the water frae the burrn. Their croft is lower, sae the gravity wud help. We could manage wi'oot a pump. Aye ... " Angus was impressed.

"And while we're about it, we'll build a bathroom for them ... I shouldn't think there'd be room in the croft for one, would you; so we'll add on a bathroom and we'll install a proper boiler ... you know, like Alison's. One which heats the water and you can cook on as well. Alison's always talking about it. She loves it. And if Mr. Wotherspoon makes any objections and won't stump up the money and the insurance won't either, I'll pay for it myself, or the estate can pay me back when I'm twenty-five or ... when I'm twenty-five," she repeated hastily. "I'm sure Mother would approve of me spending money on the estate. It does seem wrong," she added reflectively, "me with that lovely castle all to myself and ... well ... so <u>much</u> ... money and everything and poor Mrs. McLennan having to live in a pigsty. Oh, and when they have a bathroom, they won't have to go out in the snow to the privy, will they? Oh Angus, do you think they'll be pleased?"

"Aye they will that. It's a fine notion, Miss Bella. And Mrs. McLennan expecting another bairn, I'm tauld."

"All the more reason then. How soon can we start?"

'As soon as possible,' thought Angus; 'if it's going to bring the colour to your face and take your mind off whatever is fashing you.'

THE RETURN OF THE STONE

Keith paused outside the drawing-room door. From within came the sound of the first movement of the Moonlight Sonata, played, he realised with some surprise, as Beethoven could have meant it to be. So often it is rendered in a slipshod, or worse, soulful manner, with a slithering action, rather than the positive bonding of the triplets which form the prelude to the melody. It usually set his teeth on edge ... hating the way the left hand is so often rendered as a repetitive accompaniment instead of a theme in its own right. No mean performer himself, he rarely attempted this work, knowing he couldn't with so little practise, ever get it right. But she has, he thought. Nothing soulful about this rendering; haunting, yes; very melancholy; and there was something else about her playing he couldn't pin down ... and which disturbed him profoundly.

The door stood open a little. He pushed it wider and walked in. Isabella paused on the dominant seventh and looked up, leaving her hands on the keys, the piano reverberating with unfulfilled conclusion.

"Well, Isabella Mackenzie," he said. "And how do I find you?"

She got up and came slowly towards him. "Is she pleased to see me, I wonder," he thought ... with no idea that her heart was threatening to break loose from its moorings and bound from her body. She put out her hand and he took it in both of his. Her eyes were fixed on him; her expression hard to read. There was no light in them though.

"Have I disturbed you," he asked. "I'll go away if you like ... but I'd rather stay."

"Oh, yes. Please do stay," she answered a little

breathlessly. "How ... how nice of you to come. I was hoping you would."

('But perhaps not at that moment. Don't hurry her,' he told himself. 'She's not going to fall into your arms just like that. She's by nature a solitary person and she's got no reason to want the company of men at the moment.' A fleeting thought that she might be one of those people who are independent to the extent that they do not need, only suffer, their fellow creatures, he put from him. Perhaps he was a little disappointed by her somewhat reserved greeting, but what else had he expected on the strength of such a brief - and somewhat, for her at least, harrowing - acquaintance?)

"You're alright?" he asked again. "No more difficulties?"

She shook her head and made as if to take her hand away. He held on to it for a moment longer, then seeing her expression become a little troubled, he released it and, walking across the room, he came to rest under a long picture.

"I said I'd present you with my credentials one day," he said over his shoulder. "This is our common ancestress. Your Isabella's grandson's granddaughter. Your third great grandmother and mine. So that's how it is, Cousin Isabella. Not as direct as yourself, but I do qualify, don't I?"

"Of course you do," she replied, laughing. "So that's how it is." She came across the room to stand beside him. "Mary. Yes. I see. She had six children, didn't she?"

"Yes. And that picture, Angus told me, is by Lawrence?"

"I believe so. And that huge one of our first ancestor of all, Colin, the first Earl is by Benjamin West; and this ... " she walked over to the bookcase and pointed up to a tiny, by comparison, perfect portrait by Raeburn ... "is Keith, Mary's eldest son. Were you named after him? He was an admiral but by all accounts not a very satisfactory character otherwise."

128

"I don't know. There were lots of Keiths in my father's family."

"It's a good name. I like it," she told him gravely.

He took her to lunch at the hotel where he was staying and afterwards drove her home. He left the Bentley outside the castle and she took him for a long walk to the river ... "These wooden slats we're walking on, they're very slippery in wet weather," she told him somewhat breathlessly, for it was a steep uphill climb. "An aunt of mine - the wife of the soldier Mackenzie, who marched with his regiment and his dog, Cruiser (who's buried in the dogs' cemetery in the Dell to your left), all the way from Kabul to Kandahar. She couldn't walk and had a bath chair. In order that she could go for airings down by the river they put down these slats. She was enormous ... a great lump of a woman ... German, I think. It can't have been much fun getting her back again. It's a steep pull ... though not as steep ... as ... as up the Rock."

('Now why did she hesitate when she said that?' Keith wondered. 'And why is she blushing? Something to do with that bastard who ... well, never mind. None of my business.')

"And this is the River Walk, and here's my pool where I swam every day in the summer. You must come and fish it some time. Some of the best fishing in Scotland, Angus tells me. It's let but he'll fix it up for you."

"Ay. I'd like that fine, Isabella Mackenzie," he said, Scotswise. Isabella laughed again. 'That's the second time,' Keith thought, looking at her approvingly. She looked happier now; her cheeks were pink and so was the tip of her nose, as the day was cold. As he watched, a small drop appeared at the end. He found it endearing. 'And now,' he thought '... at last ... there's some light in those strange eyes of yours.'

They walked all afternoon, returning at dark for tea. Alison had left home-made bannocks and scones inside the door, together with a new pot of raspberry jam, and fresh butter from Isabella's herd of Friesians.

After tea they sat quietly; they talked about family relationships and she played the piano for him again - a Chopin nocturne, which Keith thought she made sound like a Highland burn in spate; long cascades of silvery sound. As he got up to go, he said, rather tauntingly, feeling that what this girl needed was a challenge: "this morning you played the first movement of the Sonata as it should be played, but I bet you can't manage the second."

"Well, I'll try," said Isabella. She went back to the piano, launching immediately into the thunderously tempestuous second movement of the Moonlight Sonata. There were a few wrong notes - Beethoven shows no mercy to his players, especially those with weak hands and little ability - but Isabella's hands were both rather large and extremely strong and she put so much into the playing that when they finally came to rest on the last chord, she looked utterly exhausted, he thought. Or perhaps it was the long walk. She still did not seem fully recovered; still tiring too easily for someone of her age.

"Oh," she said, wiping her brow with her hair as usual. "Gosh, what music. Poor Beethoven."

"Why? Apart from the deafness."

"Well, he didn't make things easy, either for himself of anyone who tried to do him justice."

"Which you did. Fine playing, Isabella Mackenzie. You ought to be a professional. Goodbye, I must go. Shall I see you tomorrow?"

"Oh, I hope so. Come and have lunch with us, Alison and Angus and me. At the Estate Office. Come here first, at about half past twelve and we'll raid the cellars for some drink. You'll only get tea otherwise."

She saw him to the door, watched till the Bentley's lights

were out of sight, then went back into the house and sat down again at the piano. But the mood had gone and she was very tired. Leaning her elbows on the keys, she stared at the music in a sort of trance.

That night she had another 'seeing'.

There had been two since she got home, both so strange that it was impossible to know whether to relate them to the past or the future. One was of a group of smallish men, bearing a strong resemblance to the naked savages of her coat of arms, only these, as far as she could see, were not black and the ragged garments they wore round their nether regions were just recognisably of the Mackenzie tartan. But they were behaving most oddly, attacking each other like dogs, without weapons, and when one went down, the victor knelt over him, his knees one on either side of the fallen man's body, pinning him down. Isabella saw one bend to the throat of the man beneath him with bared teeth, and had they not been people, Isabella would have said that the crouching man was tearing his victim's throat out. She didn't know what to make of it and, as before, it was soundless (which was something to be thankful for) and soon vanished abruptly, not to reappear.

The other 'seeing' had been of an arid landscape, disquietingly recognisable as the familiar one all round her. But gone were the trees as she knew them and the green grass of the lawns; instead there were naked stumps and the formerly green lawns were like slabs of crazy paving, large lumps of dry earth deeply scored with dark, jagged clefts. There was not a green, living thing in sight.

Then she 'saw' the river, or rather the deep cleft of its course, for there was no water. The burn had dried up too, as had the wells upon which the castle was built. No drop came from the taps and in the fields lay dotted mounds of skeletons

131

of beasts which had perished in the drought ... and such a drought. Total. It must have lasted - or was going to last - for years.

Once more the vision, then the blank, as though a reel of film had broken. Again Isabella knew not what to make of it, but apart from hoping that it was in the past rather than in the future (which would bring difficulties enough, without a total drought) she was untroubled. She was becoming used to her 'seeings' and as long as they weren't too nearly related to her, she could ignore them, or at least push them into the recesses of her mind.

But that night she had one she could not ignore. She 'saw' herself drowning in her pool in the river which was no longer of water, but of blood. There was blood flowing into the pool and out of it and she was sinking beneath the surface. The last she saw of herself before the cut-out were the clotted strands of her trailing hair as the clinging blood dragged them under.

She awoke and rolled over, her legs clamped tightly together. So that was it. Only a dream then. But it was a week too early and there was no elfin moon. 'That Stone's not doing its job properly,' she thought as she fished in the little cupboard by her bed. It was a long time since this had happened and she had learnt during the summer to rely on lunar influence.

But *was* it a dream. Had this been only a dream and not a proper 'seeing'? She put away the thought that it might be connected with the future, as she had taught herself to do whenever she could with 'seeings' and dreams ... whenever it was possible to separate them. She decided to give this one the benefit of the doubt, except that with a dream, usually whatever was happening, or about to happen, to oneself, didn't. One woke up before it could, if it was ... well, like this one. If

Kenneth Mackenzie had murdered me, she wondered, or been going to murder me, would I have seen myself before it happened?

Should she tell Keith? Perhaps, when or if she got to know him better. He'd probably laugh and he didn't believe in her Stone and anyway it was none of his business ... or not yet. Safely padded, she fell asleep again.

After lunch Keith said:

"You're looking tired. No long walk today. Doctor's orders. I'm taking you for a drive. Where shall we go?" And before she could reply, he said: "Will you show me the place where the other Isabella found the stone?"

"But ... " she exclaimed, stammering a little. "That ... that was at Chanonry Point. In the Black Isle."

"A nice distance for an afternoon's drive then. Besides I'd like to see Chanonry Point. Isn't that where the Burning took place?"

She could not account for the feeling of extraordinary discomfort which came over her at his words. The Burning. Screams. Fire. 'I see the Fire,' had cried the Seer, and for a moment she was there in that haunted place and all round her were the smells and the animal noises of the mob, and the air was thick with smoke and the smell of tar and burning flesh ... and the screams ...

She came out of her trance to see Alison and Angus and Keith all looking at her; anxious and unhappy.

"I'm sorry," she gasped. "I ... did I say anything?"

"No, dearie," replied Alison. "But Doctor Mackenzie is right. You look very tired, my bairn."

"I didn't sleep very well last night. I ... I was trying to memorise the second movement," she said looking at Keith, hoping she sounded more convincing to him than she did to herself. She gave herself a little shake. "Bless you Alison," she said, bending to kiss her. "After all that lunch, how could I not be fine? And ... yes ... I'd love to go to Chanonry Point. I've never seen it. There's never been enough petrol for outings, has there Angus?"

"Are you sure?" asked Keith at the gates, as he waited for a slow tractor loaded with turnips to make its ponderous way out onto the road in front of them. "We needn't go to Chanonry Point if you don't want to ... perhaps it was silly of me to suggest it ... ?" He raised an eyebrow at her questioningly.

"No. It was me being silly. Of course I want to go. It was just that for a moment I thought ... I thought ... "

"What?"

"I heard screams," replied the girl bluntly. "And I smelt it all ... all the smells of the Burning."

"You're too imaginative," he said gently. ('And you're still in that highly nervous state common to women who have just had a termination of pregnancy.' But he did not say it aloud.)

"Perhaps," she answered. "No, not perhaps. Of course I imagined it. Just as I imagined all the others ... except the murders. They were real."

But for her sick dread of what she might hear - or see - or what might happen - at Chanonry Point, Isabella would have enjoyed the drive much more. Keith drove well, but there were few stretches of road where he could really let the Bentley rip. Most of the roads were narrow and as pot-holey as the ones round the castle, and they were often held up by plodding farm horses or ancient tractors trailing plumes of blue smoke.

The Firth looked cold and grey and mist blotted out the horizon. A long narrow road bordering the little bay and dotted with crofts mostly uninhabited led them down to the Ness, or shore.

Isabella climbed reluctantly out of the door of the car

and onto the running-board. She would have liked to stay in the big, friendly car as though by so doing she would be protected ... the forces of evil kept away a little longer. What she expected to see ... or hear ... she didn't know. Perhaps she half expected the Burning re-enacted, and Keith noticed she kept pulling nervously at the ribbon round her neck as though she wanted the stone in her hand.

"Go ahead," he said, looking at her.

"Go ... what?"

"Take out the stone if you want to. It may keep the Evil Eye off you for a bit longer."

"Oh, you are a beast." But she fished it out from her jersey, opened the neck of the little bag and slid the Stone into her hand.

"Well ... it is silly, I know ... but if nothing happens here ... the scene of the Burning, then I shall know ... " She stopped.

"Know what?"

"That in a way, the matter has been taken out of my hands and I'm not responsible. Mainly perhaps because it'll mean it's all partly my imagination. Only partly because so much of it is real, but I shall have more control over this ... this thing ... power, if you like ... which seems to have taken over my life."

Keith nodded, though he was far from understanding. He looked across the Ness to the sea.

"Is this the actual place? Where, exactly?"

"I don't know. Nobody does; nor even if it ever happened, but it must have been close to where we are standing, because there isn't all that much room, especially when the tide is in ... and there were a lot of people. Here, perhaps. Or just over there? Isabella spoke of a castle, but I don't see one, or the remains of one do you?"

They walked to the edge of the sea. Isabella took off her shoes and paddled until Keith said her legs were as pink as a flamingo's and if she stayed in the water much longer, she would lose all the circulation in them. Then they played ducks and drakes with bits of sharp slate and all the time her fingers were playing with the Stone. Normally unimaginative, yet something from their common ancestry must have come to Keith, for he too felt the menace of this lonely place.

It was getting dark. Night had already fallen on Inverness and the Firth's southern shore and it was cold.

Back in the car Keith asked:

"Nothing happened, did it? No screams? No groans? Hae ye lost the power, Isabella Mackenzie?"

"I wish I had. You know, for all that he was evil, I have some sympathy for the Raven. It must have been most uncomfortable for him too ... all that 'seeing' ... and so often the wrong things at the wrong moment."

"Hm." Then, his voice suddenly serious, he said:

"Put it back, Isabella. You can do without it now. You said so in London."

"What? Oh, the Stone. Where I found it ... in the drawer of the bureau do you mean?"

"No. Here. Where <u>she</u> found it," and as she did not answer, he said carefully: "Such things can be dangerous ... like spiritualism and out-of-body experiences and such. All forms of magic are dangerous unless you can be sure of the upper hand."

"Which you don't think I've got?"

"At the risk of offending you ... no. Not at the moment. Look; give it to me. I'll take it down to the edge of the sea and return it to where it ought never to have left."

"No. It's got something to tell me and I <u>must</u> know. Something to do with the future which only concerns me ... at least only I can bring it about, whatever it is. There's still something I must do and only the Stone can tell me, whatever

136

horrors it's got in store for me. Besides, <u>it's</u> not evil. It helped
the Police, or would have done if that accident hadn't happened.
No, it wouldn't," she corrected herself, "because they'd never
have believed me. But there was a time when it made me very
happy. Happy and contented. It doesn't matter. It was nice
anyway ... while it lasted."

"And what did it do for the two Kenneths?" enquired
Keith. "It was the undoing of both of them. One because it
gave him the idea he was the chosen servant of someone or
other, and the other because it seems to have turned him into a
murderer."

"You're not serious about this, are you?" she demanded.
"What about all the prophecies then? You do know them?"

"I've read Alexander Mackenzie's book."

"Well then. The Seer 'saw' things that he couldn't possibly
have known would happen, but they have. Railways; cars;
canals ... as well as Isabella's husband up to no good in Paris."

"Knowing Seaforth as well as he did," said Keith dryly,
"that shouldn't have put too much strain on his powers."

"Oh, you're impossible. Such a cynic."

"Perhaps, but in the 17th century how *could* he have
foretold all the other things?"

"How could Leonardo da Vinci have foretold - to the
extent of making detailed sketches of the aeroplane or the
helicopter (which is still in the prototype stage here) ... or the
bicycle? Do you think perhaps *he* had a stone too?"

"Stumped," he said cheerfully. "You're quite right of
course. Many mechanical things were known of long before
there were engines to run them."

"Well, then?"

"There could be an answer," he said slowly. "It is just
possible that neither Leonardo nor the Seer are unique. To some
people ... a very few ... it is given a sort of sense of extended

logic. For example, if you admit that we are still evolving, then it makes sense that some things, mainly essential ones like communications, medicine and so on will either expand in practice more rapidly than others, or are easier to understand and foresee. I'm putting this badly ... it's a bit metaphysical and outside my scope ... but if you take certain things - bridges for example, *they've* come a long way since Stone (or Iron or Bronze) Age man threw a log across a stream too deep to ford. Some things have just progressed to accommodate others. Better roads for faster horses drawing lighter and better-sprung carriages and coaches, which have both come a long way since the days of the wooden cart of Saxon times. And the horses themselves have evolved; quite different from the huge draught horses of King Arthur's day. Some things obviously had to wait for three centuries - even more - to happen, but that's not to say someone hadn't thought of them before. Leonardo da Vinci sketched his and so we are the wiser. The Seer used his stone and credulous listeners recorded his prognostications, but, to a certain type of mind, a logical follow-on - or evolution - of ordinary present day things is normal. There were iron railway tracks some time before there were engines to run on them, though that's possibly not a very good example. And didn't he 'see' steel too? Long before it was as it is now?"

"What stopped them all from happening sooner?"

"I suppose, though the broad outline of the plans was there and sound enough, there wasn't enough expertise to co-ordinate and follow-up. I mean, even though iron was in use very early on, steel hadn't been invented so the railways - anyway - were for the future. Aeroplanes even more so. I wish I knew more. All this is just surmise."

"If *you* had that sort of mind, like the Seer, what would you see?"

"In medicine? Oh, a sort of progression from penicillin

... some drug which suits everybody. And perhaps the separation of cells which cause genetic diseases. Oh, and isolation of germs which are the cause of so much infant mortality ... scarlet fever ... that's gone, thank goodness, but only just. But of course, it's all coming."

"How can you be sure?"

"Because we're still evolving."

"So the Raven's 'seeings' were all ... what was it? Logical progressions of thinking?"

"I believe so. Except perhaps for the final one."

"He foretold the end of the family," she said her voice melancholy. "And he's supposed to have said: 'And of the Castle not one stone shall remain.' But I think Sir Walter Scott wrote that. He knew all about the prophecy ... the family one ... he was there when it happened."

"If the castle's not repaired fairly soon, that's what will happen," Keith said, trying to get a laugh out of her. He did.

"Oh, you are hopeless. We've been waiting for the Ministry of Works or someone to come up with some compensation for the mess the military made of it. That should be here soon and we can start on the roof, Angus says, when we've enough slates. They're quarried in Aberdeenshire and you can see for yourself what a lot we need."

"Yes. It's late, Isabella. I must take you back." He paused: "You won't let me put the stone back?"

"Not yet. I'm sorry, but as I told you, the story isn't finished yet."

"Alright. But I hope ... oh, I don't know. I think you've infected me with your forebodings. Is it a 'frith' ye'd put on me, Isabella Mackenzie?"

"No. No 'frith'. I don't like them." She told him about the grisly relics in the shed at the croft. "That was a ;taighairm', a sort of 'frith' ... a Druidic spell, really. Like the spancel."

"Charming! You're well rid of that one. And if you weren't I'd come back at night to your castle and you would let down your long hair for me to climb up and rescue you, Isabella Rapunzel?"

"Do you treat all your patients as though they were silly children?"

"Yes. No. Depends. But my patients, dear silly child, are expecting me. One more day with you, then I must go back to London."

"Oh ... oh ... must you? Yes, of course you must ... and I must get on with putting the furniture back in its right place ... except where the roof leaks. Old Wotherspoon had an endless list made when the military arrived, so we know where everything should be ... more or less."

"Well, don't you go lugging heavy furniture about just yet, will you? I'll be back soon, you know - if you want me, that is. What time shall I come tomorrow?"

But the next morning early as she got cautiously out of bed, she experienced the sickeningly familiar feeling that her entire insides were dropping out of her into the crackly knickers which she wore to protect her beautiful linen sheets. They were made of rubber, like mackintoshes, and with much washing they soon became stiff. Then they tore and were useless and made noises like toy pistols firing when she moved. They were hot and uncomfortable, but while they lasted, they worked. But when she felt in the cupboard for a couple of the heavy duty cotton-wool towels which were the only ones of any use to her at that stage, there were only two left. Of course Keith had warned her that she would be irregular for a while after the operation; of course, thinking about him, she'd forgotten it. How could she have been so careless and what was she going to do? She'd been so certain that there was another unopened

140

package. Walking stiffly - much padded - jerking her legs like a puppet, she got herself down the passage to the 'throne room' as Alison called it; took everything off with extreme caution and sat down. The sudden rush of blood shocked and thoroughly frightened her. It had often been bad, but never as bad as this, except after the operation. But then there had been someone to help her. Now she was alone. Even if with her remaining ammunition she could get as far as the linen room and find some old bath towels (and there were plenty of those) by now she was so alarmed, she didn't dare move. She really was in a muddle. Isabella began to cry.

The tears running down her long nose, she bundled up the gory mess on the linoleum at her feet into pages of old newspapers and put them into a bin. This she'd have to take down to the incinerator in the courtyard as soon as she could, and embark on the laborious process of burning its contents. It always took ages. Either it was raining, or the matches were damp, or the wind so strong that even in the courtyard surrounded by castle, it usually managed to extinguish the feeble flame as soon as she lit the match. Old candlestick ends were kept till they were a pool of wax because they were so difficult to get. Paraffin was burnt to the last drop in the oil lamps which were her only source of light during the long power cuts which never lasted less than three hours, and usually more.

Very cautiously she rose and, supplementing her painfully inadequate existing protection with Bromo (not very absorbent, but better than Izal) she made an improvised bundle of herself again, blessing a quiet interval. She had stopped crying and sniffing sadly cleared up and crept back to bed. She wouldn't be able to get up today; no chance ... and probably not tomorrow either and Keith was going tomorrow. She began to cry again.

She made herself stop crying and blessing the telephone

by her bed which Angus had had installed for her (priority: young girl alone in vast house) dialled the number of the hotel. A sleepy voice said Dr. Mackenzie wasn't up, she didn't think, but she'd knock on his door and tell him he was wanted.

"Oh please do," begged Isabella, distraught as another slithering rush made her break out in a sweat of fear. "Could you tell him it's Miss Mackenzie - from the castle ... and it's urgent ..."

"Ay, I will so, Miss Mackenzie. Hauld the line, wull ye?"

"What's happened?" came his voice after an eternity of waiting (she was not to know he'd come down the stairs three at a time).

"I can't get up ... I've got ... you know ... THAT," she stammered, all the old embarrassment coming back; hating it, its name, all three of them. Everything to do with it.

"I wondered yesterday. You were so pale and fidgety. Is it bad?"

His calm voice steadied her. "Yes ... rather. And I've run out of THINGS ... I forgot to buy any. I didn't expect ... " her voice rose slightly hysterically.

"Well, you are a one for the euphemisms, aren't you?" He heard her gulp, beginning to cry again.

"Don't worry, I'll get everything you need; just tell me what."

She told him the name and the size and when she said four packets, she heard a long whistle down the telephone.

"Heavens. Are you preparing for a siege in the future?"

"No. The siege is now." Her voice shook.

"I'll be with you in about twenty minutes. Can you hold on till then?"

"I think so. But the shops don't open till nine."

"The chemist will when I tell him I'm a doctor. And I'll get something from him which will calm it all down. Just stay

142

still and DON'T WORRY.

He came through the door, crossing the floor to her bed in a few strides as soon as he saw her pale face on the pillow almost hidden by the high collar of her nightdress. He put the parcel down beside her and sat down, taking her hand.

"Poor Isabella. But it'll be alright, I think. We'll know more when you've had a few of these," and he turned her hand over and slid two pink pills from a little white box onto it. "Take 'em now. You've got some water I see. Good. Now we can calm down and think a little."

"It'll be alright, I think," he said again reassuringly. "But if it hasn't steadied by this evening, you might have to go to hospital and be curetted."

"Cur ... what?"

"Scraped. As you prefer euphemisms you'll find if you have to have it done, they'll refer to it as 'tidying-you-up."

"As though I was a room or a cupboard or something. How horrid. I don't want to."

"Well, I don't think it'll be necessary. But you will if I say you must. It would be dangerous not to. There's something left in you which is causing irritation to the lining of the uterus ... or would you prefer me to call it the 'family coach' as my mother used to?" Isabella giggled weakly and he smiled at her "... and that is what is causing the trouble, I <u>think</u>. But these pills are a great help. They cause strong contractions ... to the FC ... and that helps to expel whatever it is causing the irritation. But they are strong and may give you a pain."

"I shan't mind if they work. What brought it on?" she asked. "It's never been so bad ... at least not since ... since ... oh, dear," and more tears rolled down her nose into her pillows.

"Don't cry," he said fondly. (He hadn't meant to sound so - at least not yet. But she looked so sad and forlorn and

143

alone in the huge bed; alone in the world, and it wasn't much too soon, as he was going away tomorrow; anyway he hadn't precipitated anything. It had just happened a bit sooner than he had intended - wanting to be sure.)

"Don't cry," he said again. "You're not going to die. I'll see to it personally that you don't. It honestly does happen quite often after a termination of pregnancy, especially with someone with your colouring. But you really will be alright."

"This time ... but ... " (She wanted to tell him of the 'seeing' of herself drowning in the deep pool in her own blood.) "Of course," she agreed.

His eyebrows drew together, and she thought as she'd so often thought before, not just how kind he is but how <u>lovely</u> he looks. Deep-set, very blue eyes and brown, only slightly crinkly hair. A distinguished nose, rather long like her own and strong, <u>good</u> hands. She thought he was looking rather worried, and hastened to reassure him. "I did have a dream, only because ... because THIS ... was about to happen to me anyway and ... well, I'm sure it was only a dream. But I do wish I didn't have such horrid ones."

"You're too much alone, Isabella Mackenzie. And you haven't been well ... among other things. And that stone has been giving you ideas."

"They're not ideas exactly. They're ... well ... visions. I <u>told</u> you."

There was a short silence. Then she asked timidly. "Will ... will you stay with me for a little while? Even though we can't go out?"

"As if that makes any difference. Of course I'll stay with you. You don't imagine I'm going to leave you here alone in this state." And seeing her smile, almost happily, he said: "no wonder you've got a death wish; you're wearing a shroud. Premature, I assure you. Put it away until it's needed, which won't be for a little while yet, I shouldn't think."

He got up from the bed as she laughed out loud and walked round the room inspecting the furniture and the pictures. She watched him contentedly, her eyes never leaving him as he went from object to object.

"This house is a treasure trove," he said, "the insurance must be a nightmare though."

"I don't know. The trustees see to all that."

He came back and sat down on the bed again. Almost without realising she did so, she stretched out her hand to him. He took it and held it in a warm, comforting clasp, watching her intently.

She dropped her eyes, not wanting to appear brazen; not wanting him to know she was in love with him; fearing to embarrass him because he could not possibly be in love with her. For all she knew about him, which was very little indeed, he might be married. Gently she took her hand away, pretending to need it to find her handkerchief.

Still he watched her; then he sighed.

"I wish I hadn't got to go back to London tomorrow and leave you."

"Oh ... I'll be alright tomorrow, I expect. When will I know?"

"By this evening."

"Oh ... good." (Relative good only. 'I want it to get better, but oh, I don't want him to go.')

He got up. "I'm going up to the Estate Office to see Alison and get some breakfast for us, and I'll bring lunch as well, then we can be peaceful. Alison knows you're not well and she's probably got together a gargantuan feast for us. You know what she is."

"Yes, indeed. Bless her. And you must pillage the cellars ... you've no idea how huge they are ... row upon row of bottles.

You might find something you like. The inventory is there somewhere."

" ... if I don't freeze solid looking at it. The first thing I'm going to do when I get back is to light an enormous fire." He looked meaningly at the one-bar electric fire sitting dwarfed in the huge grate. "An *enormous* fire," he repeated. "I won't be long."

He went away and Isabella's eyes followed him to the door.

He stayed with her all day. He found champagne in the cellar and insisted she drank it, bringing with him two Jacobean glasses which were part of a set he'd found in the drawing-room. They were dusty, so he polished them to a shining brilliance with the edge of a sheet, then held them up to the sun to admire the rainbow colours in among the delicate carving.

With the champagne went cold pie and jam tarts and coffee out of a thermos. Afterwards Isabella prised herself from the bed with extreme caution, put on her plaid and, extracting a packet from the parcel Keith had brought her, tucked it under the plaid. He was next door admiring the bath set in the middle of the floor of the dressing-room and its attendant geyser which either produced cold water, a trickle of scalding water, or nothing at all except spiders and earwigs, whereupon it blew up.

"Emmett," he said as he held the door open for her. "How he would love that geyser. And the bath. No hole in it I see. I suppose some luckless housemaid had to bale it out."

She returned and as she got back into bed he stood up from the hearth from whence the fire was producing a very creditable blaze, and asked professionally: "How is it? Any signs of improvement?"

"Yes, I think so. Yes, I'm sure."

146

"Another ... no; better make quite sure. Two more pills, then. No pains?"

"Hardly at all. I don't really notice them when ... " she was about to say 'when you are here', but changed it to "When I've had so much champagne."

She lay flat and after he had built up the fire he took off his shoes and came to lie beside her on the counterpane which she never took off completely because it was so heavy, usually rolling it up and pushing it aside at night and hauling it carefully back in the morning. Now it lay between them.

"Oh bother this thing," he grumbled. "I can't even see you."

"Take it off then; but Keith - it's very old and tears even if you only look at it."

"I'll be careful," he promised. He gathered it up easily and laid it over the back of a sofa. "Lovely. But it comes between us and I can't allow anything to do that, however lovely and old and valuable and all that."

He lay back on the bed. The November sun was very low and touched his dark brown hair to gold glints and showed her in strong relief, the fine features (which she hadn't liked to stare at too openly) so typical of the race. He looked like a Mackenzie - certainly recognisable as one, as too are the Frasers; the Campbells; the Ogilvys; the Roxburghes; all their descendants tend to family likenesses and the Mackenzies are no exception. Isabella Seaforth certainly had it and she was no import, having been a Mackenzie of Tarbat. "He has her ... and my ... nose," she thought, "but his isn't so long."

He sensed her gaze and turned his head. Then realising how soon he was going away, she started weakly and silently to cry, still gazing at him with a look that seemed to have desperation in it.

Immediately he sat up, moved over to her and folded her

147

within his arms, holding her to him with great gentleness and a complete absence of passion. That would come later ... if it were going to. In the meantime their minds were one and the rest could wait.

In his odd moments he gave much thought to the peculiarity of female psychology. 'What's she really like?' he wondered as she lay quietly against him, equally as passionless. ' ... when she's free from the aftermath of this recent experience? What was she like before? Where do I come in? How can I help her to deal with this stupid stone thing?' And, finally, the most searching of them all, 'will she ever accept me sexually?'

Isabella had no idea of what was going through his mind. Her face was pressed into the rough and hairy Harris tweed of his coat. She left it there until a particularly long whisker tickled her nose and she sneezed. She moved away a little.

"Oh dear," she said sadly.

"I'm not going for long. And when I come back I am going to ask you to marry me."

She gasped; then asked shyly: "Why not now? I'd feel safer."

"No. If I asked you now, you'd probably say yes, and that would be taking a most unfair advantage of you. You must think about it. Obviously you are a solitary person by nature, and marriage won't change that. You never know you might find it extraordinarily tiresome not being on your own. And so, Isabella Mackenzie, you have got to be absolutely certain that you want to marry, and that you want to marry me. After all you hardly know me."

"That can be remedied and I certainly don't want to marry anyone else."

"Still, you must think it over very carefully. The answer may be 'yes, but not yet'. You will want an heir of course, but there's plenty of time for that and you must not be hurried into

... " he broke off, not quite sure how to phrase what he wanted to say. He met her eyes and realising what he was referring to, she dropped hers quickly.

(Yes. A stumbling block - and possibly a serious one. That <u>bastard</u>, he thought with a violence wholly untypical.)

"If we married," she said slowly, "I wouldn't necessarily need an heir. You are a true descendant and then when ... if ... well, you could marry again and ... "

He took her by the shoulders and shook her slightly.

"Isabella, you're to stop this nonsense. You are not going to die ... not today, nor tomorrow, nor in the foreseeable future. Why ... what makes you talk like this? Is it just the aftermath, or have you really got a proper, valid reason ... and I mean both proper and valid for supposing this thing? If you're not careful you'll wish it on yourself. It's all because you will wear that terrible garment. Haven't you got any proper nightgowns? Pretty ones?"

It was a shame to worry him so much. She made up her mind with real heroism never to tell him about her horrible, drowning dream. And it was only that ... nothing else at all. So she smiled at him lovingly:

"I like my shrouds, Keith. They're warm and they're quite pretty really." She held out a sleeve for inspection. "Look, lovely lace and embroidery." He caught her to him again and they remained for a long while thus.

Whoever wrote 'parting is such sweet sorrow,' thought Isabella savagely, had obviously never experienced one like this. It was not a sensation she herself was familiar with, having usually been the one to go away and never having been sufficiently fond of anyone to mind losing them. But this was different. She missed Keith so much it was a physical pain, as though huge teeth had bitten a great lump out of her, leaving

149

her flesh raw and quivering. It was only made just bearable by his frequent telephone calls for which she was always ready, sitting on her bed half an hour before the appointed time.

They arranged to meet in Edinburgh ten days from now so she could see another doctor, a friend of Keith's, about the haemorrhaging and she could then take him to visit Mr. Wotherspoon and tell him her news: 'That is, if he hasn't changed his mind about me,' she thought, melancholy as always when she was tired. As for the new doctor there was nothing to be done there. She knew that with absolute certainty.

But at twenty-one, her health steadily returning, and as the days went by with bearable swiftness, she cheered up and was soon able to help Angus go to market and oversee some furniture moving. She still tired easily and the thought that Keith might not get back before the next onslaught was always at the back of her mind.

She thought constantly about him, trying all the while to equate her new situation with her curious 'seeings'. Since the drowning (the Burning; now the Drowning ... even the words were similarly strange and prophetic), the vision had returned again but only faintly. But of course, as she now realised, she had been deluding herself. It had not been a dream. But why was it so faint the last time? "Is it a sign that the Stone is losing its power or, a sudden cold feeling creeping over her, a reminder?"

That night she 'saw' again and it was the last 'seeing' that she would ever experience (other than the recurring one). On the steps of the castle sat a little girl of about four with long yellow-brown hair. Beside her, a book held up in both hands, reading to her, was Keith.

They were married two days before Christmas.
To Alison's disappointment Isabella refused to wear a

150

proper wedding dress. Instead she wore a woollen coat and pleated skirt with a herring-bone pattern which she'd bought in Edinburgh and with it a new black velvet beret with her caberfeidh brooch pinned to it. Keith wore Highland dress and looked rather stern, but imposing. Angus gave the bride away and Willie McLennan acted as best man. Such of her tenants as could attended (all but the very old and the babes-in-arms), but there was no reception and no honeymoon to follow upon this austere wedding. Later there would be a great gathering at the castle but now, after exchanging greetings outside the church, they went for a short drive up the strath, returning for high tea with Alison and Angus.

Later they lay together in the vast golden bed. She was cold, shivering a little in the silk nightdress Keith had bought her, missing her shroud. He took her in his arms to warm her and after a while she stopped shivering and aroused, he began to kiss her. She submitted but, as he'd feared, there was no answering passion in her. Not even an awakening or a sign. He turned away and lay on his back, his ardour quietly ebbing.

She sensed his mood; had known exactly how it would be - as it quite likely always would be. But she must make an effort. They were committed to each other and she loved him dearly. But she knew beyond any doubt, that whereas he could be hers, she could never be his. Besides (more practically) what was one supposed to do? To feel like?

She put her hand on his cheek to turn his face towards her.

"Keith," she whispered, "don't go away."

"I haven't," he said rather sadly. "But you don't ... I mean, you're not ready for me. It's too soon. And I love you. I'm not going to force myself upon you."

"It's not really too soon. This ... well ... this will be so

151

different." (It must be. It really must ...)

"Really," he asked eagerly; "you mean you want me?"

"Yes."

Later when he slept she took the Stone in her hand and moved it about in her palm. It felt cold - unresponsive. Perhaps it really had lost its power - at least the power to harm her. But what of the last 'seeing'. The child? And had she fooled him?

She hadn't of course, but Keith (only pretending to be asleep), thought it had gone off better than he had expected, which was a terrified and total refusal of her body. They could, he hoped, go on from there, even though with less ardour on his part (and obviously only simulated enthusiasm on hers) than might otherwise be expected with such a well-matched pair on their wedding night.

How could he know that not only had she no idea of how she should behave, nor of what to expect in reciprocating feeling, but that she was afraid? Afraid, with a deep primeval terror of his body on top of her repeating the crude actions of Kenneth Mackenzie. Gentle at first, he had soon become less so and then her beloved Keith, her husband, had become someone else. As his movements had become more urgent, all her fear and loathing of this horrible act returned and she was pinned down, suffocating. At that moment he was no different from (and indeed in the space of those few agonising moments he might have become ... turned into) Kenneth Mackenzie. The climax had come just as she could bear no more and turning away from her he was once more her Keith. But she was sobbing and trembling violently, her skin clammy and cold, her hair damp with sweat, and as he turned on the light he saw for a split second the naked fear in her eyes. She hid her face immediately but not soon enough.

"Darling, did I hurt you? I was afraid it might be too

152

soon."

"No. No. It's alright," (muffled). "I'm a fool. It's only that ... that ... for a moment, it wasn't you, it was ... "

He put his hand over her mouth. "That's what I meant. Too soon."

"It's alright," she said again, rather wearily. "It'll be different next time," but wondering if it would ever be different. Perhaps if she kept reminding herself it really was Keith and not ... She shuddered.

What hadn't occurred to Isabella was that Keith was almost hating it too and it was only partly a streak of stubbornness in him; partly the absolute necessity for an heir, as he saw it, which made him determined to go on; to woo her and anything else that was needed to make her accept and with luck ... finally ... to respond. But he was not a hot-blooded, wenching sort of man and she was making it difficult for him to summon up the necessary enthusiasm. He wished they didn't have to, with a very fair idea that she was wishing the same.

The only child of a gentle, philanthropic doctor and his ambitious wife, both ascetic, church-going and Presbyterian, Keith had been brought up under a repressed regime. Having no idea what he was going to do with his life, he accepted without question that he was to become a doctor like his father, but unlike his father, a country GP, he was to go on, specialise and buy a practice of a very different kind from the one he had been brought up with. This was his mother's wish, and as she was a strong-minded woman, as well as ambitious and with money of her own, she got her own way. In due course Keith was sent to Edinburgh and during the long years of graduation, he sowed such oats as he needed to. He also, during that period, found out what life could be like for the woman at the receiving end of such pleasuring and at the end of his time he'd had enough of the prostitutes of Leith and Portobello, the terrified daughters of genteel tradesmen, caught in the sexual web, and the results of the bungling efforts of the back-street abortionists. After his time in the Navy, mostly in shore establishments, he went to London, bought himself, with help from his mother, the practice in Wimpole Street, sublimated his occasional and not very strong sexual desires in work and music. Because of the knowledge he had brought with him from his student days, he did what he could to help the unfortunates who poured into the hospital in various stages of desperation, by acting as consultant there once a week, helping them as best he could; still, at twenty-nine, horrified and often saddened by the miseries endured by wretched women at the hands of men; determined that he would have no part in contributing to them.

What can they do - people in Keith's and Isabella's position?

Separately they thought about it and worried, and more than once Keith tried to discuss it with her, but though she made an effort - a painfully conscious effort - to listen, they got nowhere. She was too shy, and the subject was so obviously hateful to her that no good could come of forcing himself on her in this respect either. But he did not despair. He felt optimistically that time would bring a solution, as it always does. Not perhaps an ideal one, but a solution nevertheless.

On New Year's Day - Hogmanay - they gave a ball for the tenants in the newly refurnished dining-room and hall and Keith raided the cellars for all the champagne he could lay his hands on - dozens of cases stretching as far as the eye could see, together with some of the port known as 'Rebellion' port, which had been laid down before the Battle of Culloden. Angus, he knew, liked port and this promised to be special. Isabella and Alison brought out the Jacobite glasses and polished them to a blinding shine. Out came also the Worcester gold and yellow dinner service with the crest; the silver from the bank; miles of monogrammed linen table cloths and druggets and anything else they thought was needed to make the house resplendent after its long period in the wilderness. Nothing could make it warm, but there would be a great mass of food and they were to dance reels later on in the Hall with Willie McLennan, an accomplished piper (from six generations of them) to play for them. Only ... Isabella looked him squarely in the face when she made her request ... not Lady Isabella's Feast. She did not want to be reminded of the last time and Kenneth Mackenzie, but as Willie looked disappointed, she relented. Everything was different now and there was no point in giving cause for wonderings; whats and whys. She wished she hadn't mentioned the subject.

Such was the activity and the planning for what was to be, they hoped, an occasion no one would ever forget, that Isabella had given no thought to a dress for herself. Keith would wear highland dress. But she could hardly appear in her wedding suit and she had never needed an evening dress, nor even a cocktail one since the Surrey days. Trying on one of the few remaining, a frilly confection of flowered cotton, apart from the fact that it was now much too short, it looked idiotic. It had never suited her. "Aunt Kitty's idea of a suitable garment for a young girl; certainly not mine," thought Isabella, eyeing it scornfully; wishing she had something slinky and black and now she was a married woman; with a low neckline ... well, fairly low. But the little town could come up with nothing and it was too late for a visit to Edinburgh even if she hadn't used up all her coupons and some of Alison's too, on the Burberry and shoes and her new suit.

"I wonder if there's anything in the chest," she thought; "if not it'll have to be my tartan." She went along the passage to a spare bedroom where there were several chests, one containing the shrouds; another, dull things like mangy old boas, fichus and modesty vests; and a collection of hats, mostly black, ornamented with ragged feathers and jet beads. But there was another chest which she hadn't so far explored and it was with her head in this that Keith found her digging like a terrier, flinging old corsets and yet more shrouds out behind her. As she straightened up and sat back on her knees, her hands full of moth-eaten crepe and black lace, he dropped a kiss on her head and she looked up and smiled.

"You're looking for something to wear, I take it?"

"Yes. Nothing so far but I can always wear my tartan. You like it, don't you?"

"Yes. Very much ... but ... Oh, well; pity we didn't think of this before though, when we were in Edinburgh."

"We didn't know then; about the ball. Oh ... oh ... look ... I believe I've found something;" and she began to pull out from the bottom of the chest firstly layers of tissue paper, then very carefully, a mass of mulberry and silver satin.

She stood up, holding the dress against her. It seemed familiar to him.

She nodded. "Yes, it's the one ... or an exact copy ... she was wearing this when she was sitting for her portrait. Oh, Keith; can I wear this? I would love to ... if it's not too overdressed."

"That's for you to say ... or we could ask Angus. He's the arbiter. No, I think they'd like to see you wearing something grand, especially as it's part of the whole thing. After all, it's not as if you'd gone off and had a replica made just to cut a dash. Will it fit, do you think? If not, you can always wear your shroud."

She was already removing her jersey and skirt and stood there, tall and slender, as Keith helped her slip the dress over her head. Between them they managed what buttons they could that still remained and she went to stand before the long pier glass admiring herself.

"It'll fit in with the china and the glasses and all," he said, thinking how desirable and how dear she was.

"It's a bit tight and torn in places," she observed, twisting herself to get a better view; "and I've got much squarer shoulders than Isabella. Why did they all have those queer dropped shoulders in those days, I wonder."

"Search me. People do change shape over the centuries; grow taller and so on. Perhaps it's something to do with diet. I don't know."

"Oh, it is lovely. Keith, do you think it could be the original?"

"After nearly three hundred years? It could be, but I wouldn't think so."

"Well, I think it is. It feels so right, somehow. The only thing is, it won't come quite far enough down ... "

"Just as well; can't have them all goggling ... "

"Nothing to goggle at. Don't be vulgar. I meant, if it won't come down below my shoulders it'll be ... is ... too tight under the arms. Never mind I'll give it to Alison and she'll contrive something. There's probably a bit of stuff in the seams she can add to it. She's awfully clever. Let's look."

She spread the dress on the dusty carpet and turned the skirt back as far as the waist. She was right. Each seam had a broad turn-back and there was a piece of material in the train itself - more than enough to let into the bodice.

As she examined the dress Keith glanced curiously at the other contents of the chests all spread about on the floor. "You know," he said seriously; "a museum would love these. Perhaps not yet but one day. Rather than leave them mouldering here, wouldn't it be better ... ?"

She interrupted him, her voice puzzled:

"Darling, come here a moment. There's something odd ... look."

She pointed at one of the seams and on either side of the join he saw that a piece of mulberry satin had been cut out ... cut very carefully too ... where the mulberry joined the silver and opposite, a corresponding, identically-sized piece of silver satin had been removed as well.

"Now that's really odd," she said. "Who could have done that and what for, do you suppose? It's not as though those pieces were big enough for an alteration to the dress, is it?"

"Perhaps she burned the dress with a cigarette end," he suggested flippantly.

"Silly. They didn't have cigarettes in those days. Besides, if those pieces had been used for patching, they'd show on the skirt."

"Look in the train. That's all folded together and patches wouldn't show, though how you can burn a hole in your train unless you sat on a cigarette ... cigar, then ... I've no idea. She might have torn it, though. Darling, I must go. There's so much to do."

She blew him a kiss and went back to her inspection, but though she searched every bit of the voluminous skirt and train as well as the bodice, paying special attention to the area under the arms, she could find no trace of the missing bits of material. But she was sure it was the right one ... Isabella's own ... not a copy. All the other clothes smelt strongly of mothballs. This dress had a faint, but quite definite scent of cloves and in places it was very worn and even a little stained, especially under the arms. Isabella was touched. Somehow she could never think of

158

people from so long ago as real; only waxworks in the right clothes. 'I'll send a snippet of this to Edinburgh, one day, she thought. They might be able to date it."

She put the dress on the bed and went downstairs.

The party was a great success and even though dancing with Keith to her own reel, the Lady Isabella's Feast, might have set off something (which she was half expecting) no occult experience came to spoil it. Instead she thoroughly enjoyed it and was delighted with the remarks about her dress. It was much admired and approved of, especially when it was explained where it came from.

Both of them drank a great deal of champagne and Keith had also had a quiet session over the port with Angus in the study while Isabella was talking to her tenants. By the time the last guest had been seen off into the snow and the lights turned off, it was well past midnight.

"Oh," she said, yawning widely. "That was such fun. How nice they all are. I do hope they enjoyed themselves."

"They certainly seemed to," he replied, looking at her fondly. "Come on. Bed. You look like Lord Randall."

"Lord who?"

"He who was weary with hunting (only it's dancing in your case) and fain would have lain doon only Mother hadn't made his bed ... or something ... " She blinked at him owlishly for a moment.

"Oh, yes. I remember. And all his bloodhounds swelled up and deid. He didn't have much luck, poor handsome young man. I bet he wasn't as handsome as you are, though."

"You're completely tipsy. Come *on,* Izzy."

When he came in from the dressing-room she was in bed already nearly asleep. 'And wearing that damned shroud, which

159

I could well have done without tonight,' he thought, the champagne having made him sleepy, but not so much as to render him incapable ... if she felt like it. For once she seemed relaxed, her limbs disposed bonelessly like a large puppy instead of being all stiff and tense. He climbed into bed beside her.

"Take that thing off," he whispered urgently, wanting her; reckless; not disposed to take no for an answer.

"No," she mumbled, peering at him through her hair. "Oh, alright; *you* take it off," provocatively. But his urgency was too great; already too far out of control to allow him to wait ... or be careful. He pushed the bulky garment up where it bundled itself into a roll beneath her chin causing him to swear briefly and Isabella to giggle. But he was quick; too quick for her to automatically brace herself.

"Oh ... " he said at last, contrite. "I *am* sorry. I never gave you a chance. And no wooing at all tonight, I'm afraid. Must have been all that champagne. Still, it served its purpose."

"What purpose?" She was awake again, wishing he wouldn't talk about it.

"Well, you accepted me. Usually you stiffen up and ... well, you didn't tonight, that's all. It was so nice. Not for you though."

"Yes. Nice for me too."

"But all over so quickly." She put her hand over his mouth.

"It doesn't matter. I like it better that way," she lied. She still didn't like it at all in any sort of way, but he must never know. She added, so quietly that he could barely hear her: "I wonder if I'll have a baby now." And was asleep on the instant.

'That must mean she had taken no precaution,' thought Keith. Neither had he. 'That champagne has a lot to answer for, one way and another if she hasn't, but it's not the end of the world for all that she's too young and not properly

160

recovered.'

He'd made his gynaecologist friend in Edinburgh fit her with her 'precaution' as she called it on the rare occasions when she referred to it at all - and she hated it. It was a brute of a thing made of tough, smelly rubber mounted on a steel ring. This primitive form of contraception about the only one at that time was alright if a person could take it, but Isabella couldn't. She was the wrong shape for it or any other device. She could never get it into the right position and it hurt her constantly; when she put it in; when she wore it and when she took it out. And it needed so much attention, having to be as regularly washed and powdered as a baby's bottom. As an efficient deterrent to successful lovemaking it could hardly have been bettered.

Keith slept deeply, tired out, but Isabella woke again to the vision which she had in these last days almost forgotten. Once again she 'saw' herself drowning, her head already nearly submerged in her blood. Bitter disappointment was succeeded, after a long hour, by acceptance. At least now she could no longer ignore this vision and she had already known for some time that it was not a recurring dream. This was her fate soon. Perhaps in a year or two; perhaps sooner; some time within the next year? She had no idea. She turned over and the vision faded and went.

She kept the Stone in her hand. The little girl she had seen sitting on the steps? Had that been a dream? She didn't want to wake Keith, he was so tired, but her distress was so great ... she couldn't bear it.

"Keith?"

"Mm ... oh, I'm so sleepy."

"Never mind. Keith, I'm going to die."

He put on the light and sat up tousled and slightly alarmed.

"Darling!" He put his arm round her. "I've told you lots of times, you're not. You look perfectly alright to me," he added peering at her blearily. "No more moribund than you deserve after all that champagne and dissipation. Darling Izzy, do let me sleep."

"No. I've had that 'seeing' again. The drowning one ... " forgetting in her agitation her resolve not to tell him.

He interrupted her, "It means nothing, you know. The champagne again. Only a dream, darling."

"I thought it meant nothing the first time ... even the second ... but not again. Not now. Oh, Keith, I don't want to die until ... until ... "

"You've got an heir, do you mean? Darling, it's not that important and there's no hurry. You said you've got one ready-made in me ... anyway it doesn't *matter*. Not yet."

"It does. I didn't tell you before but I 'saw' her ... after the Drowning one."

"Her?"

"Yes. A little girl of about four; sitting on the steps and you were with her and you were reading to her. I couldn't hear of course, but you had a book in your hands and she was listening to you. She looked so like you; and me too. Her hair was exactly like mine ... and Isabella's. What does it mean, Keith? What does it *mean*? Oh, how I wish I knew."

"Knew what?"

"How much time I've got. When all this is going to happen."

"You've got a lot of time and though I like the sound of the little girl and hope very much that *does* happen ... some day ... the other you must put out of your head." He spoke as lightly as he could, deciding to be very firm as well, but he was nevertheless deeply disturbed.

"I think it will happen quite soon. All of it. It's meant to

162

happen so what's the point of waiting? You can't put off or precipitate Fate. I know that because when I saw you both, you didn't look any older than you do now. So we must ... you know ... "

"Again? I'll do my best, though I can't guarantee success. But you'll have to relax, darling, otherwise it's like trying to make love to a bolster." He was rewarded with a small giggle.

'Perhaps she'll be happier now,' he thought before dropping into an exhausted sleep, 'and not have any more of those dreadful visions.'

The following days Isabella was in good spirits, and she knew already she was in the family way, as she thought of it, because that was how it was meant to be, just as she knew the baby would be a girl. She knew also that her short, troubled life was nearly done and she had achieved, or would have done with the birth of her heir, what the Stone had shown her she must do. She wouldn't be troubled by it again, she was sure. Perhaps one day she would act on Keith's suggestion and return it to the waves. But even as the thought occurred, a blank feeling followed and she knew she would not. Fate still had work for the Stone, though she would take no further part.

As the days lengthened and winter became spring and summer Isabella grew rounder and pink again as she'd been the one before and during these months she was happy, as though the Stone had decided to exercise for a little longer its beneficence. As the days grew warmer, she became disinclined for too much activity (which Keith in any case would not allow) and spent much of her time sitting with Alison on the verandah, idly watching skeins of white wool turn into little garments under Alison's capable hands. Usually Alison brought tea and sandwiches and sometimes Keith joined them and she was completely content. Now there was nothing to do. Nothing to worry about; no disturbing visions. She slept peacefully, untroubled.

It was the seventh of September. Isabella walked slowly and heavily upstairs using the bannisters, on her way to lie down on her bed. She tired easily nowadays and her back ached as the pull on her muscles increased. It ached more than usual at this moment, and suddenly a pain of grinding intensity shot through her, doubling her up and causing her to cry out. It came again as she staggered towards the bed and fell on it, her knees drawn up, her face twisted. It passed and she could reach out for the telephone and call Alison, who with great presence of mind immediately telephoned the hospital for an ambulance, then got on her bicycle and free-wheeled down to the steading to tell someone to find Keith or Angus, before making for the castle.

The ambulance got there first. They got her to the hospital and next day, twenty-two hours after labour had started, she gave birth to a girl baby weighing six pounds. She had tried all through the long hours of labour; never giving up, but once the baby was born, she began to die and there was nothing they could do about it. Towards the end she recognised Keith; acknowledged the baby with a little nod; then made a feeble gesture somewhere close to her left ear and said in a threadlike voice, so faint that Keith had to bend close to her to hear: "Please, put it back." He felt carefully under the pillow, withdrew the Stone and put it in his pocket, no doubt now in his mind as to its final resting place.

She fixed her eyes on him and smiled and as her life went out on a dark tide; the car carrying the blood which could have saved her lay upside down in a ravine near Dalwhinnie.

164

After the funeral which, as was the custom in Scotland, was attended only by the men of the estate, Keith got into the Bentley and drove to Chanonry Point.

Leaving the car he walked half-way down the shelving Ness and looked for a long while at the dark waters of the Firth, the tide on the ebb.

He took the stone from his pocket and turned it over once or twice in his hand frowning over it. Then, with a swift gesture, back went his arm, sending the stone hurtling through the air to fall among the shingle on the edge of the sea.

A long wave closed over it and drew it back from whence it had come nearly three hundred years before.

AUTHOR'S NOTE

The Magic of Stones

Down the years, from the very beginnings of history, stones of all kinds have held a special fascination for people. Even today the 'Druids' (self-styled but nonetheless convinced) welcome the summer solstice at Stonehenge. All over the country great stones are venerated. The tors of Dartmoor and Exmoor; the 'henges'; the standing stones of Callanish in Lewis and elsewhere throughout Scotland. The Old Man of Hoy ... there are many instances where stones play their part in rites and magic.

So it was with Coinneach Odhar Fiosaiche whose 'magic' stone brought him fame, almost veneration and certainly caused his downfall. The question we must ask ourselves is exactly what part did this stone, variously described as black with a hole in the middle, blue and white, the shape of the new moon, play in the utterance and ultimate fulfilment of his prophecies.

If we believe in his existence then we must also believe that the Stone was essential to him in the prophecies to which he is attributed. Equally it is necessary to believe that he alone was responsible for the prophecies which at one time were an integral part of Highland legend. All this has been excellently documented both by Alexander Mackenzie in his book *The Prophecies of the Brahan Seer* and much later, thoroughly dissected and explained, wherever explanation is possible, by Elizabeth Sutherland in *Ravens and Black Rain*.

But explanation is not always possible. For example, did Coinneach Odhar prophesy because he was convinced the Stone gave him some power or would he have prophesied anyway?

And if so would it have been to quite such effect?

The theory that radioactivity in stones of certain kinds is transmitted to the person with whom they are in contact, causing a super-sensory state of mind and nerves to take over, is plausible, given that it appears necessary nowadays always to have some scientific explanation for odd, ghostly or otherwise unnatural happenings. But whether a small stone, however radioactive, could generate sufficient power in a person to enable him to see nearly two hundred years into the future and prophesy with such alarming accuracy the fate of an entire family, is difficult to believe. Here is where science lets us down. There ought to be a scientific explanation for Coinneach Odhar's fulfilled prophecy, but there isn't, nor is there any record of any legendary or otherwise successor to bring the prophecy a little closer to the time of its subjects and fulfilment.

I am neither a geologist nor a soothsayer, nor do I know anything about radioactivity, but a year or so ago while walking on the Ness at Chanonry Point I found a small stone, slightly blue, elliptical enough to induce thoughts of elfin moons, magic and Seers.

It didn't do much for this book because I was well over half way through before I found the stone, but the book had been heavy going. Not so its sequel, *The Watching Shadow*. Sometimes when awake for a time I would take the stone from under my pillow and hold it. Always afterwards, perhaps not the next day, but very soon, the ideas for the book came so thick and fast it was impossible to keep up with them. The whole book was written in longhand in a matter of a few weeks, between the beginning of autumn and the end. Unlike *The Seer's Stone*, this book never flagged. I even tried to put it away for a week, but it was too demanding and would not let me rest.

Now I have ideas for the third (see *The Final Prophecy*) which concerns the history of the Seer's prophecies as they affected the family of which I am a descendant. *The Final Prophecy* will be the most difficult of all. How will my stone help me, if at all? By the mere fact of owning it and its associations with the legendary Seer and the terrible death he met at the hands of Isabella Seaforth at Chanonry Point, will it inspire me? And by autosuggestion, radioactivity or what? It will be interesting, though I shall never know, if as with Coinneach Odhar, the inspiration will be there anyway, stone or no stone.

Inspiration or none, I am very careful how I use my stone. Not to summon up inspiration. That would be unwise. One might get more than one bargained for. I wait, hoping for it to happen. So far, it has given me just what I wanted and no more.

* * * * * * *

M. S. 1994